Along the
Shore Path

Along the Shore Path

CHILDHOOD SUMMERS AT THE LAKE

Chris Brownstein

New Lands Press
Chicago, Illinois

Along the Shore Path
Copyright © 2014 Chris Brownstein. All rights reserved.
MsChris324@aol.com

ISBN 978-0-9832609-5-0 (Paperback)

Cover photo by Jamison Jepson
Illustrated by Ethan Young
Book design by DesignForBooks.com

Dedication

This book is dedicated to
Isabella, Zack and Lev.
May your little feet run free on the grass.

Special thanks to
Ted Brownstein and June Van Gelder
whose tireless support has been largely responsible
for the completion of this book.

Contents

1

Tattle-Tale

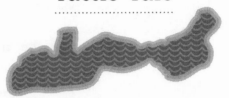

"Draw a round circle, color it purple, somebody poke!" As I lay face down on the pier, my cousin Katie ran her finger around in a circle on my back as the rest of the gang chanted. When they got to the "poke" part, somebody jabbed me hard, really hard. Much harder, I was certain, than what the game required.

"Ouch, that's too hard!" I cried.

"Oh come on, that didn't hurt!" Katie insisted.

I sat up, and looked around the circle through the tears in my eyes We'd never had so many kids around before, but that particular summer was unique. My mom had decided to take up golf, so my twelve-year-old cousin, Katie, was visiting under the guise of babysitter. Katie was a beautiful girl with long blond hair, deep blue eyes, a turned up nose and an amazing talent for attracting boys. In fact, it was her boy craziness that was responsible for the whole arrangement. Her mother believed, as all mothers do, that getting her away from the bad influence of the kids in her neighborhood was all she needed. That, together with fresh country air, a little responsibility and the presence of her innocent young cousins would transform her back to the sweet, well-behaved Katie everyone knew; fat chance with thirteen-year-old Dean Brewster in the area.

Nothing much changed during the first week, except my mother was gone a few days. Barbara and I continued to play together as Katie sat inside sulking. She hated the bugs, the itchy grass, the hot sun, and the disgusting, sea weedy lake. She wrote long letters to her friends, polished her nails incessantly, paged through her voluminous collection of movie magazines and kept her ear to her transistor radio. She'd been incensed at her exile and clearly I was the culprit.

After the first week, however, everything changed. Somehow her pheromones reached Dean Brewster, who was also young and gorgeous and might have passed for Fabian's little brother. His mother was renting a cottage over on Lake Como. How those pheromones managed to travel up the hill, over highway fifty and back down the hill to Lake Como remains a mystery to me, but I swear, they did. They were powerful enough to draw Dean, his younger brother and a whole gang of other adolescents right to our front porch. Once Katie laid eyes on him, her exile no longer mattered; neither did the bugs, the itchy grass, the hot sun or the seaweed.

They were all circled around me, staring, waiting for me to guess who had poked. I studied each face, trying to remember all of their names. Dean was easy, of course, being the oldest, the tallest and the undisputed leader of the pack, the alpha male. I could also remember his younger brother, Daryl, who was a smaller, eleven-year-old replica of Dean. Aside from the flirtatious glances between Dean and Katie, everyone remained poker faced. The faces melded together like the waves of an angry sea and I became scared and flustered. Finally my sister Barbara spoke up. "Come on! Guess! Hurry up, we haven't got all day."

I was certain that the painful poke had been from her, her way of telling me I didn't belong with her new, older friends. "It was you!" I said confidently.

"Wrong!" they all shouted. They dipped the bucket into the lake and poured cold water over my head. It was the penalty for guessing wrong. It was so cold! I began crying again.

"You didn't have to pour it over my head!" I screamed.

"We couldn't help it, you're just too short." Everyone laughed. Instinctively I turned to run up the hill toward my mother.

"I suppose you're going to go tell your mommy now. Tattle-tale!!" These were Katie's painful words, repeated by Barbara and a few others. I wasn't sure, because I just kept running. My mother suggested I change out of my wet bathing suit and then offered

me the privilege of dusting the porch furniture. I tried to do a super job, to impress my mother, but the splashing, the laughter and the screaming of the kids down in the lake distracted me. I looked down to see them playing follow-the-leader off of the diving board. They were having so much fun. "I want to go back down and swim," I announced to my mom.

"No, you stay here now and help Mommy. Let the big kids play." Big kids? Here was a new and divisive category I hadn't had to deal with before. Up until that moment Barbara had been my constant companion. How'd she suddenly fall into the category of "big kid?" She was only nine, just three years older than me. Katie and the others were three or four years older than her! Of course, I hadn't actually done the math since I hadn't learned to add yet. Still the injustice was painful.

Once Dean had discovered Katie, hardly a day went by that he didn't visit. Usually he had his brother and several other kids in tow. Sometimes they'd swim and sometimes they played games on the lawn. A few times they let me play hide and seek with them, but they used it to slip out on me, and after the fifth or sixth time I finally got wise to it and quit playing. Most days they'd pick up Katie and Barbara and disappear.

In the evening Barbara would taunt me. "Oh, you'll never guess what we did today!"

"What?" I asked, eagerly.

"Don't tell her," Katie would chime in, "She'll tell your mom!"

"No I won't! I promise!"

"Yeah, right!"

"No, really I promise! Cross my heart and hope to die!"

"Well, OK, but you understand that you really will die, right?"

"Yes, yes, yes!"

Barbara couldn't wait to tell me. "We explored the old Maytag house today. You know the one over by Buttons Bay? The door was unlocked. We just followed Dean and walked right in. We explored the whole thing. It is so cool!"

"I want to see it too!" I cried.

"Oh, it's way too far for you to walk," Katie said with her superior and condescending smile. Every day it was something bigger and better.

"We got to see an Arabian stallion!"

"We got a ride on a hay wagon today, thanks to Dean!" Katie said dreamily.

"We saw the red haired hatchet lady over at Covenant Harbor Bible camp! She almost caught us."

"We saw a boat catch on fire and blow up!"

"Dean snuck us all into the theater for free. We got to see a Bridget Bardot movie!"

"Very sexy," Katie said.

"What does sexy mean?" I asked. They laughed.

"Speaking of sexy," Barbara began, looking mischievously at Katie, "what's it feel like kissing Dean the way you do?"

"Shut up!" Katie stopped her, and darted her eyes toward me indicating that this was not a matter for my little ears. "Anyway, you and Daryl . . ." Some days they remained silent about their adventures. Those days were the worst. I just had to know what they'd done, even though every story made me drool with envy.

On the days that Katie was meant to baby-sit, my mother would always give her "the talk," telling her what she was to prepare for lunch, where to find the country club phone number, and explaining to her that her first duty was to watch me and Barbara and keep us safe. Katie knew how to turn on the charm.

She'd put her arm around me and look down at me lovingly. Then she'd give my mom her sweetest, most endearing smile, "Auntie Irma, you know I'd never let anything happen to little Sandy." Why, she was so convincing I almost came to believe it myself. My mother was thus able to enjoy many happy, worry free days on the golf course. I, on the other hand, was not so happy.

Most days Katie managed to pawn me off on the neighbor, Mrs. Murphy, which worked well for both of them. They must've had some kind of secret system between them that I could never figure out. Seems like one minute I'd be happily playing with Barbara and Katie and the next I'd find myself all alone. Suddenly Mrs. Murphy would appear with Becky, consoling me and walking me over to her house. Becky was only four and was staying with her grandma for a few weeks while her mother recovered from surgery. Mrs. Murphy was really old by this time and I'm sure Becky was a handful for her. Often she'd sit with her feet up while I kept Becky entertained doing whatever it took to keep her happy. Mrs. Murphy was very kind to me, though, so I didn't dare complain. She fed me lunch, and when her legs weren't hurting too badly, she'd let me and Becky help her bake cookies. A few times she took us to town. Once she took us to the Riviera for cotton candy, and another time she bought us ice cream cones. She took us to see *Lady and the Tramp* and even bought me and Becky each a new toy at Schultz Brothers. My mother remained oblivious to this arrangement. Barbara and Katie would always retrieve me just before my mom got home and reprimand me for disappearing. They got me to believe that I'd done something wrong and righteously promise not to tell my mom. Then they'd add insult to injury, telling me about their great adventures of the day.

This worked until the end of July when it was time for Becky to return home. Mrs. Murphy drove her back to Chicago and stayed there for a whole week. This happened to be the same week as the very important July tournament, which required three consecutive days of golf, followed by cocktails and dinner. My mother explained to Katie that the days would be much longer than usual, showed her which TV dinners to prepare for supper and promised her extra money for the extra-long hours. This was followed by a strong commendation on the job she'd been doing thus far, a big hug to Katie, and a strong warning to me not to give Katie any trouble.

On the first morning Dean Brewster came down with his clan announcing, "Hey, we're gonna explore the Chapin mansion. It's up for sale. It's empty. You comin'?"

After placing her customary kiss on his cheek, Katie put on her best pout and looked at me with disgust, "We've gotta baby-sit."

"Leave her with the old Battle-Ax next door!" Daryl said.

"Mrs. Murphy's gone."

"So, just leave her! We won't be gone long," suggested Daryl.

Katie put her arm around Dean, tossed her hair the way she always did, and looked up at him helplessly. "Ohhh, I want to see it so bad! But my aunt would kill me if anything happened to Sandy."

Barbara looked at Daryl and tossed her hair, just like Katie. "Daryl's right. She'll be OK by herself for a bit."

"Bring her along, she might prove useful," Dean said, looking down on me with his deep brown eyes and seductive smile. For one lovely short moment I felt warmth and acceptance. No wonder Katie liked him so much.

"She won't be able to keep up," complained Barbara. "She'll moan and complain all day, and you know she'll tattle about anything we do."

"I will not!" I screamed. "I haven't told mommy one single thing you did all summer. I crossed my heart and hoped to die! Remember?"

Dean towered over me and stared down with a stern face. "Is that true?" I vigorously shook my head. "OK then, you know the rules."

Barbara insisted I cross my heart and hope to die once again. Then they decided I needed to swear it with my hand on a Bible, but we couldn't find one. We settled on a church page of the yellow pages. After all those promises Katie pulled me aside and whispered, "You've got to do what we say! If you tattle about any-thing, I'll see to it personally that you die." Piece of cake. No problem. I was willing to do anything to be a part of the clan and their great adventures.

As leader of the pack Dean calmed the situation. "Hey little buddy," he said, again with the warm smile and seductive eyes, "I know just how strong you are. I know you're gonna be a great help to us, and by the end of the day, everyone will be glad you came along." That was all I needed to hear. I fell instantly in love with Dean, in a six-year-old kind of way. I was ready to do anything for him. I turned my nose up at Katie and Barbara. If Dean said it, it had to be true.

I was so proud as we marched off that morning. My first privilege was to lead the line walking through the wooded shore path, breaking the newly spun spider webs. "Hold your hands up straight over your head so you break the high ones too; otherwise we get hit in the face." Gladly I broke all the spider webs for them. Dean, with his arm around Katie, followed right after me. Barbara and Daryl held hands behind them, and four or five other kids followed after that.

The big old mansion was not far. There didn't seem to be anyone around. "Go knock on the door and see if anyone is home," Dean said.

"What do I say?"

"Just do it." So I did. No answer.

I walked back out to the clump of bushes where they were all hiding. "No one answered," I said. Dean signaled for the clan to follow him. We all walked onto the screened porch and peeked through the windows. It was still full of furniture; it sure didn't look like anyone was moving out. The door was locked, but a window had been left ajar.

Dean ordered me to his side. "Climb through here, then unlock the door for us."

"But it's too high, I can't reach it," I protested.

"I'll lift you up."

"Shouldn't someone else do it? Someone who could unlock the door better?"

"No, you're just the right size to fit through the window."

"Yeah, but, what if somebody comes? Look, there's still stuff there."

"You already knocked, no one's home."

"But what if they've got a dog?"

"He'd already be barking. I swear, I think you're scared. Come on, up you go." He hoisted me up and pushed me through till I hung on my stomach on the windowsill, half in and half out.

"I'm stuck," I cried.

"Oh for cryin' out loud!" Dean griped. With that he gave me another big shove that landed me in the great living room of the mansion. I looked at the high ceiling and felt so tiny, insignificant and terrified. I hurried over to the door, but I couldn't get it unlocked.

"Turn the top part and the handle at the same time," Katie urged.

"Come on, hurry up," they all kept saying. But I could not get it open. They were all mad.

"She's so dumb," I heard Barbara say.

"Send someone else in," I pleaded.

"We're all too big," Dean yelled back.

"Please, somebody get me out of here," I begged.

"Go find a different door," Katie yelled to me. "God, my aunt's gonna kill me," she said quietly to Dean.

"Don't worry about it," he whispered, and then I heard him plant a big old kiss on her cheek. The group was walking off of the porch, and I knew I was really alone. My heart was pounding. I looked around the big dark room. The furniture was mammoth. There was a big pipe organ at one end. I stood frozen, listening. I heard no more footsteps, only the ticking of a large grandfather clock. I got a hold of myself enough to look for another door. I walked into the kitchen. There I saw dirty dishes in the sink and bananas on the table. It was quite obvious that someone was living here. With relief I saw the kitchen door, but just as I was reaching for the handle I heard a car door slam. I ran back into the living room and hid behind one of the big chairs. The kitchen door opened, and I wet my pants. I was so scared. I thought my heart would jump out of my chest. I heard footsteps and then a lady

called, "Come on Heidi, come on. Good girl." This was
followed with barking. Heidi stood at the entrance to
the living room growling and barking her head off. She
knew I was there. I clenched my teeth, held my breath
and waited for her to chomp her teeth into me.

The lady yelled, "Heidi, stop barking!" She followed the dog into the living room, and opened up
the door that led to the front porch, the same one
I'd been unable to open. Instead of coming after me,
Heidi ran outside barking. "It's OK, Heidi, just some
kids running down the lake path." I guess the clan had
stayed around after all, but they were running away
now. I just stayed frozen behind the chair. After a
while the lady reentered the house, followed by Heidi.
I thought for sure Heidi would find me this time, but
she followed her owner into the kitchen. I think she
gave her a dog biscuit. After a while I heard footsteps
going upstairs and heard the little clang of Heidi's
tags following them. The front door was still open. I
tiptoed over to it and ran out onto the screened porch.
The porch door slammed behind me, but I didn't stick
around to find out if the woman heard it or not. I ran
all the way home. The gang was sitting on our front
porch playing spin the bottle. They seemed kind of
glad and relieved to see me, but a little annoyed too. I
was really angry and ready to scream at them for leaving me, but once again Dean took charge.

"Wow, come here! Let me shake your hand. Here
she is, everyone, the bravest girl in Lake Geneva!" He

held up my arm and turned me around to face everyone. Everyone cheer!" And they did. Then he asked
me how I got out. My heart was still pounding from
fear and from running all the way home. It took a
while before I could even talk. But once I began I was
the center of attention. Everyone sat around listening
to my adventure. Maybe the whole thing had been
worth it. I felt accepted at last.

The next day Dean decided we needed to discover
the origins of the dry creek bed that ran past the same
mansion. I wasn't nearly as excited about going with
the clan as I'd been the day before, yet this adventure
seemed completely innocent and safe by compari-
son. The day before I thought I'd proven to the group
that I was brave at least, and I thought I'd gained a
measure of acceptance. But the truth was that they
were all angry that they'd not gotten to see inside of
the mansion, and clearly it was my fault. I believed I
could redeem myself, so while I was not anxious to go
anywhere near Heidi's place again, I didn't complain.
The first part of the trek was wonderful. The creek led
away from the lake, past caretakers' cottages and into
the woods. I was keeping up just fine and we were all
confident the creek would lead to something exciting.
The land rose dramatically ahead, and then we came
to a big pipe.

"What we need," Dean announced, "is for someone to climb through here and tell us where this goes.
I'm way too tall myself." He looked around at the

group, and then the whole group was staring at me. "You know you're really good at this sort of thing. I'm so glad you're with us." He smiled at me, convincing me of every word coming from his mouth. But, crawl through *there*?!! I looked around at the faces hoping desperately for a savior. Katie looked a tad bit worried, but kept quiet. Barbara looked smug. I was terrified, but tried not to show it.

"You want me to crawl through *there*?" I asked hoping for a lighter sentence.

"You're not scared, are you?" asked Barbara, then looked toward Daryl for confirmation.

"Of course she isn't!" said Dean, shaking his head. "She's the bravest girl in Lake Geneva, remember?"

"Oh, yeah, that's right," they said, catching on to his tactics. Suddenly they were all throwing compliments my way. It was irresistible.

Dean put his hand on my shoulder, and gave me another influential smile. "It won't be long. You'll see light soon. When you get to the other end, shout. We'll all wait right here until we hear you. Just shout good and loud."

I hesitated, staring into the blackness. Then I heard Barbara whisper to Daryl, "She's such a baby, we shouldn't have brought her."

"What choice did we have?" Katie whispered back.

I stooped down and began crawling. The first part was dry and I was determined to prove myself. Steadily and carefully I moved one hand and then the other, one knee and then the other. I was beginning to relax just slightly when my hand got into some muck. I worried about frogs, spiders, snakes or rats. I tried not to think about them but suddenly both my hands and knees were in cold water. Something slithery crossed my hand. I let out a little scream. I hoped they hadn't heard. I could see nothing ahead. I was suddenly gripped by terror, frozen in place. I began to cry, but tried to do it quietly. No one could see me. The voices of the others were growing quieter. Then I heard a loud, deep voice, "Hey you kids, this is private property. Get out of here!"

I heard Dean's diplomatic voice, "Sorry sir. We were just frog hunting." Then I heard feet thumping away. I stayed there, frozen, for what seemed like an eternity. But I realized that the caretaker had saved me. I wouldn't have to finish my perilous trek. I'd simply turn around and crawl back out. How relieved I felt! Until I tried to turn around and realized that the pipe was too small to turn in. I panicked. I was stuck. I was sure the kids would never tell anyone where I was, and nobody would ever be able to find me inside. Horror on horrors ran through my mind. Would I die of hunger, thirst, or just plain cold? How many days and nights would it take for me to die? I'd never see my mom or dad again, or my grandparents either. I cried, longing for my mother. I derived some small consolation thinking that at least Barbara and her friends would feel guilty for the rest of their lives.

Then the cold was really getting to me. I screamed in panic. The echo was terrifying, but only to me. No one else heard. Suddenly I felt really guilty about having crossed my heart and hoped to die. My Sunday school teacher had told us we should never say that because hoping to die was really bad. Now I could see why. I guessed I was being punished, even though I hadn't tattled. I just lay there and cried, waiting to die. Then I remembered something else I'd once heard in Sunday school, so I started praying. I knew the older kids would've made fun of me for this, but I didn't care at this point. I stopped crying long enough to catch my breath. I calmed down enough to realize that, in fact, I wasn't stuck. I could simply crawl out backwards, the same way I crawled in. So I began one slow movement at a time. I counted each step. I thought only about the numbers and wondered if it would take me a hundred movements to get out. But it was only about ten, or maybe fifteen before I was out of the water, past the muck, and back onto the dry part of the pipe. I could feel the warm air and smell the grass. This gave me courage and I quickly finished backing out never so happy in my life to see blue sky! I sat there crying for a long time. Then I picked myself up and followed the creek bed down to the lake. I washed the mud off of my hands and my knees. I got my shoes soaked, but at least they were clean.

When I got back to the house the whole gang was playing baseball on the lawn. I was so angry at them, I'd made up my mind I wouldn't talk to any of them. But as I approached the house they all made a big deal over me. Ben, one of the boys who never said much of anything, told me I was the bravest girl he knew. Dean put me on his shoulders and paraded me around the yard. Everyone cheered. Katie brought me a bottle of root beer and they let me have all the rest of the chocolate chip cookies. They let me play baseball with them, letting me have as many strikes as I needed. When one of the pitches finally managed to run into my bat I ran around the bases while they kept fumbling the ball. I made a homerun. They cheered and went on about how athletic I was. I was just gullible and needy enough to swallow the whole thing.

On the last day of my mother's golf tournament, Dean decided we should all walk to town. That seemed like a nice safe adventure to me. Maybe someone would buy me cotton candy, like Becky's Grandmother had done. It was a long walk for me, but I never let on how tired I was, I kept right up with the others. Before we reached the stores, Dean informed me that I was to steal a pack of cigarettes in the drugstore. I didn't want to do it. I remember the lady that worked there had given Becky and me free candy just a few days before. "But that's stealing!" I protested.

"No, no, it's not stealing. See, my mom goes in there all the time. She spends loads of money there. I bet your mom does too. And Ben is going to buy something. All you'll be doing is reducing the profit margin."

"My mom doesn't get margarine there. She brings that up from Chicago."

"It's OK." I didn't really get what Dean was saying, but I didn't want to let the others know I was too stupid to understand. We'd learned about prophets in Sunday school, so I guessed maybe it was OK. Still, I was scared.

"But, I don't think I can. I don't know how." Barbara and the others rolled their eyes and shook their heads.

Dean remained cool. "Just grab one, make sure it's Winston, the red package, and slide your hands under your sweat shirt." He had me practice with a stone. "Excellent! You'll do great, and don't worry; we'll keep the cashier busy." We proceeded to Main Street and walked nonchalantly into Arnold's Drug Store. Dean schmoozed with the nice young cashier who was totally distracted by his charm, while the rest of the gang milled around the drugstore.

"Now! Grab it!" whispered Barbara. I grabbed a pack and slid my hands under my shirt.

The nice lady who'd given Becky and me candy was stocking shelves. She smiled at me and asked, "Are you OK? You look a little worried."

"She's fine," answered Barbara, as she led me out. We waited out front for the others.

We walked down to the waterfront park, and sat under the big willow tree. I loved that tree. It was a cool day and no one was around. Everyone dumped out his loot. I couldn't believe all of what they had.

I handed Dean the pack of Winstons. "Hey, you did real good!" he smiled at me.

"Nuh-uh! She just about blew it for all us," Barbara complained. "You should've seen the scared look on her face."

Dean was not to be defied. He gave her a look that shut her right up and I felt proud. He smiled at me again, and gave me half a candy bar as a reward. While I ate, Dean and Katie lit up. It was so weird to see her smoking. The others, including Barbara, stole a few puffs. No one offered me one, and I didn't ask. I was shocked and scared, but I also felt grown up. I was sitting in the park in a circle of big kids. I'd been part of their adventure.

I woke up pretty cocky the next day. I was certain I'd earned my way into the world of the "big kids," so when Dean and Daryl came waltzing up to the house the following day, I marched right out to greet them. "Where we going today, big buddy?" I asked Dean confidently.

Before Dean could answer, Katie stepped out, threw a glance over her shoulder to make sure my mom couldn't see her, and gave Dean a little kiss. Barbara yelled back to my mom, "Mom, Katie and I are going for a walk."

"OK," she yelled back as she waded through her piles of laundry. The kids headed up the hill and I began to tag along. Barbara looked at me sternly. "You can't come along. Mom is home today. You need to stay with her."

"But I want to come with you!" I protested.

"Look, Sandy," Katie tried to explain. "Look, it's me and Dean, and Barbara and Daryl. See. Just the four of us. Get it. You can't come!"

I looked at them, coupled off, holding hands. "Oh, you mean like in the movies, like 'sexy'?" I asked ignorantly. They roared with laughter.

"Yep, smart girl!" Dean said.

"But I'm useful, remember? I'm brave. I can do things for you. You'll be happy I came along."

"Get lost!" Barbara finally shouted. "You are nothing but a stupid, pesty little kid!" With that I couldn't hold back the tears anymore. "And don't go running off to tell Mommy! You crossed your heart and hoped to die, remember?"

I wanted to run to my mom's arms and cry my heart out. I wanted to tell her every detail of everything that had happened all the days she was gone. But, Barbara's last words haunted me. I had, indeed, crossed my heart, hoped to die and even sworn on the telephone book. One near death experience was enough for me. Still, I needed to get back at them in some big way. I climbed up the hill after them spying discreetly for a little while. I saw Katie and Dean kissing, just like in the movies. Barbara and Daryl were kissing too, though they looked more like woodpeckers. They'd walk for a while and then kiss some more. I quit following after a short while and returned to the house determined I would get revenge, but I hadn't a clue how I would do it.

I tried to get my mom's attention, but she was going ninety miles a minute, washing clothes and cleaning the house. The best she could offer me was to hand me a dust rag. I pretended every speck of dust was somebody's head. Eventually my mom shut off and put away the vacuum cleaner. She had to run into town and I'd get to ride in the front seat and go along with her.

As we were driving, I figured it was as good a time to ask as any. "Mommy, what does 'sexy' mean?"

She looked at me surprised. "You're a little too young to talk about that. I'll tell you about that when you get older."

She was ready to drop it there, but I wasn't. "I just need to know, because some of the kids were talking about it."

"Well, forget it, they shouldn't be."

I had no choice but to let the matter drop. We stopped by to get some groceries and popped into Arnold's Drug Store for some things. There was that nice lady again. She said hi to me, asked me how I was, and gave me a big smile. Then she took my mom aside for a minute and talked to her privately. I was really scared.

On the way home my mom asked me, "Were you and the other kids in the drug store yesterday?" I couldn't lie about that, that lady remembered me!

"Did you know that some of those kids stole some things out of there?"

Gulp! "Well, um, . . ." I never was a fast thinker, "Um." What a dismal choice; I had to outright lie, or die from tattling. "No, Mommy, no, no! Dean's mom buys butter there, see?"

"They don't sell butter."

"No, no, I mean that other stuff, margarine."

"They don't sell that either." Clearly I was incapable of getting the point across to my mother. If only Dean had been there, I knew he'd have been able to explain it. I said no more, hoping she'd just forget about it. After a little while she asked me, "Tell me, what were the kids saying about sex?"

Clearly, I needed to calm her down, get her mind off all this stuff. "Nothing! It's OK mom. You don't have to tell me because I know what it is."

"You do?"

"Sure, it's what Dean and Katie do." Oooooops! I hadn't really meant to tattle, it just sort of slipped out. After that we rode home in total silence.

The frosting on the cake came when Mrs. Murphy stopped over. She'd returned from the city with a beautiful doll for me, thanking me for all my help with Becky. My mother was a little perplexed, but I beamed as Mrs. Murphy rambled on and on about what a nice girl I was and how much time I'd spent over there.

Katie was on the train for Chicago the very next morning. Without her pheromones to draw them, Dean and his gang quit coming. Barbara made one or two attempts to hike over to Lake Como on her own, but she never reconnected with the gang. My mom hired some decrepit old lady to watch us on her golf days, though she mostly watched TV. It was a sadder Barbara, but I had her back to myself, and that was all I cared about.

Still, when Becky came back up, and Mrs. Murphy asked me to come over, I gladly went, and felt great evil pleasure at leaving Barbara to sit by her lonesome little self with the decrepit old babysitter.

2

Lost Shoe

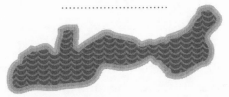

"**C**ome on, quick, we're going to the meadow," Barbara informed me. I hadn't even eaten breakfast yet, but I quickly obeyed. I loved the meadow, and I loved being part of Barbara's adventures even more. "Mom's being so mean!" she complained. I had heard my mom yelling from the other room, but had not personally experienced my mom's wrath on that particular morning. Still, I didn't dare question Barbara's decision. Being her confidant and accomplice made me feel grown up and special. Besides that, she'd become my mom's babysitter, and it was wise not to cross her.

It was a brilliant, sunny October Saturday. Our parents had picked us up right from school the afternoon before and we'd driven straight to the lake cottage. We'd gotten there in time to get a glimpse of the beautiful fall leaves, but hadn't had enough time before dark to go out and do any exploring. I knew Barbara would come up with something special. I was so happy it was Saturday, and even happier to be at the cottage. I hated my big, fat, scary first grade teacher; I hated sitting in a desk all day; and I hated letters and numbers. Barbara grabbed a loaf of white bread, a jar of peanut butter and a butter knife out of the kitchen and tied them up in her jacket. "That should do us, let's go," she whispered.

"Mom and Dad are going golfing, shouldn't we say good-by before we go?" I whispered back.

"No, you idiot! Come on, quick!" We silently slipped out the kitchen door while our parents finished dressing for their 10 am tee off time. I could hardly keep up as Barbara stormed up our steep driveway. We spoke not a word until she slipped off onto a narrow dirt path that led through the woods. "We're safe now, we can slow down a little." She was breathing hard, as I was. Then a big smile crossed her face, "I bet they don't even know we've left!"

"Why are we sneaking away?" I finally asked.

"Because that's the way you run away from home, stupid."

"But why are we running away?"

"Because Mom is so mean! You know her and Dad don't really love us. They only want to play golf."

I wanted to deny it. I wanted to argue with her, but she was right. Ever since my mom and dad had taken up golf they did nothing else, and even when they weren't golfing they talked of nothing else. I thought back over the last day. Since they had picked us up from school, just the afternoon before, it seems they never stopped yelling at us. First it was all the hullabaloo over the little tear in my new dress, then they yelled at us for the slap game we were playing in the back seat, then for singing *One Hundred Bottles of Beer on the Wall.* They wouldn't even let us continue when we changed it to coke, in fact, they ordered us to be totally quiet, not to sing or speak another word. They refused to stop for ice cream, even though we were starving. They made us eat tuna noodle casserole for dinner. They wouldn't let us play outside after dark, and they made us go to bed early even though it wasn't a school night.

"Will running away make them like us more?" I asked.

"Oh you ask the dumbest questions! We're running away. It doesn't matter now."

"Well, I wish you'd told me earlier 'cause I would've grabbed Billy, my bear."

"You can't carry a bunch of junk with you when you're running away." I resented her calling my bear "junk" and I resented it even more when she pulled the big peanut butter jar out of the jacket and handed it to me. "Here, you've gotta help carry some of the food. I carried the whole bundle all the way up the big hill."

My excitement over our little adventure was definitely dampened. The situation was scaring me, and part of me wanted to run back to the house and check all this out with my parents. I wanted to know more about the love thing. But, I knew they were in a hurry and probably would have yelled at me for asking. I was kind of curious about where we'd be spending the night and stuff. I hoped running away meant I wouldn't have to go back to school on Monday. I also wondered how soon we were going to get to eat, as I was already feeling hungry. I was afraid to ask, though, thinking these questions might make Barbara angry. For a long while we walked on silently under a magnificent golden canopy. Finally I broke the silence with what I thought was an intelligent question, "Barbara, how do the leaves turn color?"

"It's very complicated. It has something to do with the colder weather. We studied it in school, but you're too young to understand it yet. So I really can't explain it to you."

I tried to catch some of the brilliant leaves as they tumbled to the ground. The peanut butter jar encumbered me. "Do you think they'll all be down by next week?"

"Probably."

"I can't wait to see how it will look with no leaves at all!"

"Well, we'll get to now. But Mom and Dad won't get to because they won't be coming up again until spring."

"Why?"

"Because Big Foot Country Club closes after this weekend." The prospect of us being up here without them was scaring me more than a little, and I was feeling angry at Barbara.

"What a stupid name! Why'd they name the country club something so stupid?"

Barbara explained, "It's named after an Indian chief who used to live there. His people were the ones that first made the lake path. But he had to move his family away to Oklahoma so the golf course could be built."

"That's not fair! They had to leave because of that stupid golf course?" I felt really sad for the Indian children. They must've felt sad too. I wondered if they had walked through these woods and if they had liked them as much as I did. I wished they still lived there; then my parents wouldn't have been able to play golf.

We passed an old cottage that had been abandoned for years. "Do you think anyone ever lived there?" I asked Barbara.

"Of course. Somebody did. In fact, there used to be a girl who lived there. She was about . . .," Barbara paused and looked at me, "about six. Her parents were gone a lot and one day they just never came back. She lived there alone for a while. She would come and beg for food all the time. Mom used to give her cookies. But then the police came and got her and made her live in an orphanage in New York."

"What was her name?"

"Um, I think it was Annie. I was pretty young when she used to come around so I don't remember it exactly." I thought about poor Annie in that dark, dreary little cottage all by herself. I ran over to it and tried to peek through the dirty windows. All I managed to see was an old rusty refrigerator standing open. Barbara still hadn't told me where she planned on living.

We finally came to the place where a little grassy road led off the path and up toward the meadow. There was an old stone bridge at its entrance. One day last summer, when Barbara and my cousin Katie were being especially mean to me, I'd spent a whole day there waiting and crying for my mother. The grassy road led us along a hillside and deep into the woods. "SHHHHHHH," Barbara ordered, although I hadn't been talking. We stood frozen. I didn't know which way to look and I didn't dare move.

"Did you see that?" Barbara finally broke the silence. "It was a woodchuck!" I hadn't seen or heard anything, but never questioned Barbara's keen abilities. I was glad she'd seen it; I wanted her to be happy. The road led directly to a barbed wire fence, with a big, round hole that we could slip through easily. Then we had to amble through some thick woods and climb over another barbed wire fence. I'd gotten to be quite adept at this. I hoped to impress Barbara. Then we plowed through some more weeds, baby maples and some sumac bushes, until we suddenly emerged onto the big grassy meadow. It reminded me of the meadow in the Bambi movie.

I yelled, "The meadow!" and bounded off like a fawn, leaping through the deep grass. After running in circles for a while I stood beside Barbara. "Hey, can we eat yet?"

"No! This food has to last us a long time, you can't go eating it already."

I was sorry I'd asked and tried to think of something else to say. "Hey, do you think they used to keep horses up here?"

"Sure. It's obviously a horse pasture. Years ago they had a lot of horses here. One of them won the Kentucky Derby. That was before you were born though. Hey, let's play horses."

I was the baby horse. I loved my assigned role. I went running off whinnying all the way. The meadow was draped over a large hill, and dotted with treed islands. Although it was bordered on three sides by roads, these were not visible from any part of the meadow. Young trees and sumac bushes grew in along the fence lines making the meadow into our own gigantic and private playground. I was running along when my saddle shoe fell off my foot. I thought it was very funny. I looked at it lying in the grass. I went to find the mother horse, who had galloped off over the hill, to tell her of my dilemma. When I found her I told her in horse language about my lost shoe. We galloped back to where I thought I'd lost it. We galloped to several other locations as well. We finally had to abandon the horse language and speak in English.

"How did you lose it?" Barbara asked me, panting and annoyed.

"I was just running, and it fell off my foot." I didn't dare to tell her I'd actually seen it and left it lying in the field. Clearly I should've just put it back on my foot then.

"Well, where were you?"

"I thought it was over here, but then, it all looks the same." We tried to follow the paths we'd worn through the long grass, but ours, together with those of the deer, created a complicated maze that led nowhere. We looked all over, but we couldn't find it. I loved my saddle shoes. I'd worked hard for them. They'd been my reward for learning how to tie. I could feel tears welling up inside me, as I remembered going to the store to buy them with my mom. I thought about how mad she was going to be, but then realized that I might never see her again. The tears began falling. I missed my mom; even a good scolding would have been welcomed. Barbara did her best.

"Oh stop acting like a baby! I can't believe you lost your shoe! That is just the dumbest thing. How are we supposed to run away now? I wish I'd just left without you. I could've done so much better without you tagging along!" She picked up her jacket along with the bread and peanut butter and angrily began walking back home. I had to go more slowly; first of all, because I couldn't see very well through my tears; and second, because I had to be careful where

I stepped with my one shoeless foot. Barbara didn't wait for me.

I'd hoped my parents would still be at home, but they were already gone. The house felt so empty. I was mad at Barbara for not waiting for me, and she was mad at me for botching her plans. I was afraid she might just take off without me. I didn't want to be left alone, but I didn't really want to run away from home either. I took off my one good shoe and threw it on the floor next to where Barbara had flung off her jacket. I found an old pair of tennis shoes and put those on, even though they were too small for me. Barbara was making a peanut butter sandwich out of the smashed bread. I made one too. I was famished by this time. I poured myself a big glass of milk. I was happy to have a working refrigerator. We sat without talking for a long time. I didn't want her to be mad at me. I wanted her to be happy. Finally I suggested, "Hey, let's take out the blocks and build houses for our dolls."

"Sure," she unenthusiastically agreed. We dumped out all the blocks and began construction. Barbara decided that her dolls had no parents and fended for themselves by gathering wild berries. I was not allowed to copy her ideas, so I gave mine a wicked stepmother who sent them to bed with no supper at all. I was just getting into the game when Barbara announced, "It's too nice out to play inside. Let's go out and play baseball. Just leave the blocks out, we'll get back to them later."

I couldn't catch; I couldn't throw; I couldn't bat. I wished my Dad were there to teach me. Barbara wished Katie and all her friends from the summer were there, then we could've had a real game. I kind of missed them too, even though they'd mostly been mean to me. We gave up on the baseball idea. I wanted to go fishing but the pier had already been taken in. We took a short walk along the lakeshore instead. No one was around. I suggested we sneak up and peek into the windows of all the empty summerhouses, or go find the red haired hatchet lady at Covenant Harbor, but Barbara seemed to have no courage at all without the bigger kids around. There weren't even any boats on the lake creating an eerie silence we weren't used to. We returned to the house and turned on the TV, but the only clear channel we could get had boxing on. "You be the big fat guy," Barbara said. "You've got to do what he does. I'm the taller guy." I didn't like this at all, especially when the tall guy planted a great punch on the fat one and Barbara followed suit.

"I don't want to play this," I cried.

"You're such a baby!" She turned off the TV in disgust. "So what do you want to do?"

"Do you want to play Monopoly?"

"I hate Monopoly, and you don't know how to play anyhow." Of course I did when Mom helped me, but Barbara was right.

"Bingo?"

"We brought the game back to Chicago, remember?"

"How about Old Maid?"

"It's no fun with just two people," she sighed. Again, we sat in silence for a while. I was afraid that at any moment she would jump up and resume her running away plan. I had to come up with something to keep her with me.

"I know," I finally said, "let's go to the schoolhouse to play." The schoolhouse was about a mile away. They had a great tall slide, a fast merry-go-round, and wonderful highflying swings. Barbara agreed somewhat reluctantly. The walk brought us back up through the

golden canopy and past Annie's cottage. "I wish we could see in there better. Do you think her toys are still in there?" I asked.

"She probably didn't have any. Her parents were really mean." At least our parents weren't that mean. I thought about my dolls and all the blocks we'd left scattered across our cottage floor. With my hands unencumbered I once again attempted to catch some of the falling leaves. I got Barbara interested for a short while and we had a catching contest. Later on we passed a horse pasture and Barbara elaborated on how she and Katie and the other kids had fed and petted the horses there during the summer. Further on we got a glimpse of the lake with sunbeams dancing off of it. They made me feel happy, but the wind coming across was cold. I wished I'd remembered to wear my jacket. When we finally got to the school we began by peeking in all the windows, comparing this school with ours. The desks, the globe, the flag and the pencil sharpener all looked familiar. "Do you think Annie went to school here?" I asked.

"Who?"

"You know, Annie, from the little cottage."

"Probably. But let's not talk about her anymore."

We methodically tried out all the equipment, all the really fun things, and even the not so fun things like the sand box. And then we were done. The shadows began to grow long, a chill drifted in. It felt like time to leave. We were still lonely. The prospect of walking back past Annie's cottage and returning back to ours felt even lonelier.

"Hey!" Barbara's face lit up again and I knew she had another wonderful idea. "Let's walk to Big Foot!" It was brilliant. I couldn't wait to see my mom and dad. Last summer we'd walked there using the lakeshore path, so we were confidant we could go the distance. We imagined that, once we got there, our folks couldn't help but be proud of us for hiking ten miles. We didn't go by way of the lake path because we were out on the highway. Back then Highway 50 was an old, shoulderless two lane highway carved between hills with a three foot cement wall right up to the edge of the road. There was no room to walk along the road, not even for two small girls. We walked along the top of the hill instead, along barbwire fences that were bordered by thorny vines and weeds. We plowed through them, tearing our pants and scratching our hands. It was slow going. We expected that conditions would improve, so we kept forging ahead. The sun seemed to be going down at an alarming rate.

The first star popped out. Barbara began, "Starlight, star bright, first star I see tonight, I wish I may, I wish I might, have this wish I wish tonight," and then she wished that it wouldn't get dark before we reached the country club. She had me do the same and so we kept repeating it, over and over, wishing for the setting sun to pause long enough for us to complete our journey. We kept pushing forward. The scratches on my hands burned. I was tired, hungry and cold, but I didn't dare complain. I had to keep up.

Darkness descended upon us despite our desperate pleas to the first star. And then, a horrid sight, whizzing by us at 65 mph went my parents. We screamed at the tops of our lungs. "MOM, DAD STOP!" We screamed and screamed but they couldn't hear a thing. So much for hiking to the country club! Now we had to tromp back through all the vines and brambles. It was a long way. By now it was pitch black and we were growing hungrier and colder by the minute. After what seemed like hours we made our way back to the schoolhouse. There was one warm welcoming light. We rested under it for a bit, hoping we might feel its heat.

"Do you still wanna run away from home?" I asked. "Because if we get home Mom's gonna kill us. We're really gonna get it for staying out after dark. And when she finds out about my shoe she's really gonna kill me. Maybe we could just sleep here, on the school steps." I was that tired.

"Yeah, she is, but we can't run away now, it's way too cold. Besides, we left the bread and peanut butter back home. Come on, let's go. It'll be easier walking now. We know this road really well, and we've only got a mile left."

We'd never walked it at night before, and this was a very dark night. We were comforted every now and then by light that shone from the few houses along the way. In other areas we practically had to feel our way. I was scared of the dark. I was scared to go home. Suddenly these things didn't matter. There were car lights approaching from behind. If it hadn't been so very very dark we might've jumped into the bushes and hid, but it all happened before we had time to think. Instead of just whizzing by, the car slowed and stopped. We froze, like deer, staring into the head-lights. Then Barbara yelled, "Run!" She took off like a jack rabbit and I followed for few short steps until I tripped and found myself flat out on the pavement. I curled up into a ball, clenched my teeth and prepared to be kidnapped.

I heard the car door open and a familiar voice, "Sandy, stop screaming! It's me, Vivian." She was one of my mom's friends. I ran to her arms crying. She yelled to Barbara who was totally out of sight, but still within ear shot. "Hop in the car you two, I'm taking you home." The heat in the car felt wonderful; I sat in the back seat shivering. I hadn't known just how cold I was. We were asked all kinds of questions, which Barbara answered the best she could. I fell fast asleep.

The next thing I saw were the flashing red lights of a police car. I was sure they'd come to tote me and Barbara off to some New York orphanage. Someone was opening the car door, but it wasn't a policeman. It was my dad. He lifted me out and gave me the big-gest hug I'd ever gotten in my whole life. He carried me into the house where my mom was sitting and sobbing with a crying Barbara on her lap. Then I was in her lap as she continued to sob and hug both of us. Somewhere in the midst of all this the police and my mom's friend were thanked profusely for finding us and bringing us home. It was all sort of weird, because we weren't lost, and we would've found our way home, eventually.

Later on, when my mom would tell her friends about it, she'd explain how she and my Dad had arrived home to a dark and empty house. Jackets were strewn on the floor. Toys were left in the middle of a building project. There was a shoe, one shoe. Their imaginations had gone wild. My mother envisioned the kidnapper grabbing her girls. She imagined me screaming, crying, and calling out in vain, "Mommy, Mommy!" She imagined Barbara fighting for our survival. She'd have punched, hit, bitten, yelled. But all to no avail. He'd have overpowered her. No one could have heard our screams. She feared she'd never see her beloved children again. Newspaper headlines flashed in her mind, "Young Girls Disappear" or "Bodies Found." My dad had walked up the hill, calling our names. He had walked along the shore path, calling our names. He yelled, he cursed. He kicked the blocks. One of them called the police.

I can't say how long we sat sobbing on my mom's lap. By and by she heated up a can of split pea soup and we devoured it. Bed never felt so good as I snuggled under piles of blankets with Billy the Bear. The next day my parents cancelled their golf games. They played baseball with us. They played Monopoly with us. We went to town and got cheeseburgers for lunch and each of us got a new toy. My mother never said a word, no not one single angry word, over my lost shoe.

On the way back to Chicago they let us sing *One Hundred Bottles of Coke on the Wall* and we stopped and got ice cream half way home. When Barbara and I were finally alone together, just before we went to sleep, I said, "I wish we didn't have to go to school tomorrow. If I hadn't lost my shoe, we might still be up in Lake Geneva, playing in the meadow. Are you still mad at me?"

"No, it's OK," she said, "It's not a good time of year to run away from home anyway. We'll have to wait until next summer."

"Yeah, OK, but I think maybe Mom and Dad do love us."

"Yeah, maybe you're right.

3

The Deep Dark Cave Mystery

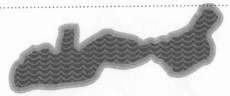

"I just found a cave!" Barbara whispered to me, all out of breath. Her clothes were covered in burs and prickers. I could tell she'd been ambling up in the woods.

"Really? Where?" I shouted.

"Shhhhh.," she reprimanded, looking around to check our parents' whereabouts. It's up in the woods, just up past the field with the apple trees. I'll take you there if you promise not to tell anyone about it." I felt her secrecy was unnecessary, but it made the whole thing so much more exciting. Sharing Barbara's secrets made me feel special and grown up. Besides, our parents were capable of turning our greatest fantasies into boring facts and deterring our greatest adventures through frivolous restrictions. Discretion was probably a wise thing.

"Of course, cross my heart and hope to die!" I promised. Visions of Tom Sawyer's cave danced in my head. I'd been dreaming of cave exploration ever since I'd seen the movie the previous winter. Would there be thieves and criminals hiding out back there? Would we get lost for days and come out heroes? Would there be glistening stalagmites and stalactites in there? I'd seen pictures of caves like that. "When can we go?"

We left immediately. As soon as we'd gotten out of hearing range of the house I began badgering her with questions. "How deep is it? How many miles long is it? Where does it come out? Is there water in it? Do you suppose there could be diamonds in there?" She became quickly annoyed with me and explained rather harshly that she'd not been inside yet. She'd been waiting for me to go in with her. That made me feel very important and I marched on proudly. But my pride was soon squelched by fear and apprehension. "You don't think there's any bears in there do you?"

"No, stupid, there's no bears around here."

"Well, what about snakes, or bats or things like that?"

"Do you want to go or don't you?"

"Of course I do."

"Then just shut up for a while." We continued the journey in silence, climbing up the hill, through the field and past the apple trees. I picked the tiny green apples and stuffed them into my pockets, planning ahead, just in case we got lost in the cave for a few hours or even days. Wild raspberries were plentiful at the edge of the woods. I figured it was prudent to gorge myself on them. I wondered if the cave ran under that very spot where we were standing, or if it plunged straight down through the earth.

"Come on, let's go," Barbara urged me after she, too, had had her fill of berries. I shivered with excitement. This would be the final stretch of our trek.

We trudged on through woods I'd never explored before. They were thick and hard to pass through. Mosquitoes badgered us. After what seemed like forever she suddenly shouted, "There it is!" I walked up to a cement wall with a little round hole carved out of it. The hole had a cross of rebar in it, resembling a window like the ones we drew in school. It appeared as though the exposed part of the wall itself had been dug out from the side of a small hill. I cautiously approached the hole and yelled down into it, "Hoo, hoo." It echoed back, "Hoo, hoo." It smelled musty and the air felt damp and cool. It looked nothing at all like Tom Sawyer's cave. I tried to hide my disappointment. "How do we get in?" I finally asked her.

"I haven't found the entrance yet, I waited for you 'cause I knew you'd probably be able to find it." She knew how to flatter me. We walked all around the area hoping to find a way in, but all we found were pricker bushes and mosquitoes. "These woods are so thick, it will take us a long time to find the entrance," she tried to reassure me. We finally climbed up the little hill to where we figured we were on top of the cave. There we found a perfectly round hole looking down into the cavern. "There! There you go!" she shouted. The dank musty odor suggested we were looking down into the same area we had just viewed from the rebarred window. I yelled into it repeatedly, enjoying the echo.

"Stop! You want to cause a cave in?" she asked angrily.

"Oh, come on!" I yelled. My disappointment, anger and mosquito bites were getting the best of me and I finally lost it. "How can I cause a cave in when this isn't even a real cave? Real caves are made of rocks, like in Tom Sawyer. You lied to me!"

"Have you ever seen a real cave?" she asked.

"No, but . . ."

"Well, then, how do you know what a real one looks like? You can't just believe everything you see on TV." We'd certainly heard those words before. "Besides, there's different kinds of caves ya know. And, if it's not a cave, *Smarty Pants*, you tell me what it is?" I so wanted to come up with an answer, not only to satisfy my own curiosity, but to impress Barbara. I was not ready to let go of the cave idea; visions of Tom Sawyer still danced in my head. From the top of the cave, looking slightly down hill, we thought we saw the roof of a farmhouse. I wanted to go closer, and maybe find a road to lead us out, but Barbara didn't want to go near it. Instead we picked our way back through the thick weeds.

After a long silence it suddenly hit me. "Hey, I know! That cement thing was built over the cave to hide the opening. They didn't want anyone to find it."

A far-fetched idea, but one I really liked, and Barbara did not reject. "There must be a good reason why they hid it." On our way out of the woods our curiosity burned worse than the nettle we encountered. I was relieved when we made it back out to the apple trees and the grassy meadow, but I couldn't stop thinking about the cave.

As we were eating breakfast the following morning, Ian, the caretaker knocked on the back door and handed my mother a jar of raspberry jam. "Oh thanks! The kids will love it." With that she opened the jar and insisted we spread it on our toast. It was really good! "Is this homemade?" she asked.

"Of course! It's a great year for raspberries. My mom put up 24 pints already this summer."

"I didn't know anyone still did that."

"Really?" He laughed a little, but then added proudly, "My mom also puts up peaches, applesauce, tomatoes, beans, corn and pickles. By mid-September the root cellar will be full of jars and also enough carrots, squash and potatoes to keep us going all winter."

Barbara and I suddenly looked at each other. "Root cellar!" we whispered in unison.

The matter might have been dropped there, but the conclusion was so dull and boring we refused to believe it. Surely if it had been a simple root cellar there'd be some old jars around or old bushels or something, not to mention a door to get in. If only we could see in there we could know for sure. We checked out our flashlights but not a single one worked.

"We need a really strong flashlight," Barbara said. "How much money do you have?"

"I got almost five dollars. Why?"

"Because we need to get ourselves a really *good* light. I've got about a dollar and a half. If we put our money together we'll have enough."

"But I was saving it up to buy that big teddy bear at Schultz Brothers."

"Well, do you want to find out about the cave or not?"

"Well, yeah, but . . ."

"Well then, it's settled. Let's get to town right away."

"Should we pack a sandwich," I asked, anticipating the hour and a half walk each way.

"No time for that. We need to get on with this." We put on our shoes and headed along the shore path to town. It was glorious at first, the lake calm as glass and not a cloud in the sky. Soon our shoes were soaked with dew, and our clothes, despite our youth, were soaked with sweat. As we progressed, so did the sun, along with my hunger. We reached Covenant Harbor Bible camp where kids were swimming, splashing and diving in the cool lake. I longed to be a part of it instead of trekking to town in search of a flashlight. By the time we reached the Riviera, the beach was packed with more wet, cool and happy

kids. I wanted to stand and watch, but Barbara moved me along. We trudged up Broad Street to Main. Town was hotter, sunnier and smellier than the shore path had been. The smells of popcorn, hamburgers, cookies and kolachy from Bittner's bakery tantalized us. We guzzled water from the nearby fountain and stared in at the delightful sweets. "Do we have enough money for lunch?" I asked, hopefully.

"Don't be ridiculous." We tried Moore's Hardware first, right on Main. Adults were complaining about the record breaking heat and discussing the Farmer's Almanac predictions. They warned each other to be careful of heat stroke. Our mission seemed to take on greater importance in light of this adversity. Barbara asked the man where the flashlights were and told him that our dad needed a really bright one for a special project. We chose the biggest, of course, one with a very long handle, and a huge head. Surely it would do the job. It needed six sized D batteries, which we also had to purchase, leaving us with just a handful of coins.

We stepped back out into the hot sun, dreading the walk home. Nevertheless, we were satisfied that we'd found the flashlight of all flashlights and soon we'd be discovering all kinds of amazing things down in that cave. We walked past Schultz Brothers where I cast a quick glance at the big stuffed bear in the window, the one that would never be mine. I waved good-by, tormented by a feeling of disloyalty. As we approached the Riviera the smell of cotton candy got the best of me. "Do we have enough money to buy cotton candy?"

Barbara counted it up. "Fifty-two cents. Yeah."

Just as we were approaching the cotton candy stand, however, Barbara had a better idea. We went over the sightseeing boat office and found out we could get a ride home for twenty-five cents each, since we were under twelve, and would be riding a relatively short distance. I'd hoped we'd get to ride on the Polaris, by far the prettiest sightseeing boat, but it wasn't scheduled for another hour. Instead, we got to ride on the Marrietta, not our favorite, but it would get us there. It felt so good to sit down, and once the boat began to move, the breeze was delicious. I watched the happy swimmers at the beach and at the camp, satisfied that I'd soon be one of them. We watched the shoreline passing by, proud that we'd walked it, proud and relieved that we'd found a way not to have to walk it again.

Soon we were being dropped off at our pier. We heartily thanked the driver and waved good-by to all the tourists. I wanted to dive into the lake with my clothes on, but I knew they'd never dry before my mom got home. We ran up the hill to change. Barbara soared ahead of me and was already pulling out bread and peanut butter by the time I got through the door. We slapped our sandwiches together and devoured them along with a couple of bottles of root beer. "You ready to go," Barbara asked me.

"Yeah, let's get our suits on."

"No, I mean to the cave."

"No, I'm going swimming. I can't wait, I'm so hot."

"But you just ate. You've got to wait an hour anyway, by that time we'll be at the cave." We believed in that rule more firmly than any religious doctrine we'd ever been taught. To swim right after eating was to invite disaster.

"But if we wait an hour we'll miss the Polaris! We can just put our feet in and splash ourselves, or maybe just float in the inner tubes."

"Too risky. I can't believe we're this close to seeing the inside of the cave and you want to splash in the water like a baby. Well, you can if you want, but I'm going to the cave now."

I hesitated for a split second as she started out the door. She knew I wouldn't tolerate her seeing it first. "Wait, I'm coming!" Reluctantly I followed her up the big hill, looking back longingly at the lake. The sun was still high in the cloudless sky, still breaking heat records. The cicadas were screaming. We didn't stop for berries. Finally we entered the shady woods where the torment of the sun ceased and that of the mosquitoes and nettle began. Barbara insisted I take my turn carrying the flashlight, giving me only one good slapping hand. It was heavy with its six D sized batteries. We'd worn a bit of a path through the worst of the weeds; so at least the going was a little smoother than the first time. Finally we saw it. At that moment I felt with all my heart that our efforts would pay off. We saddled up to the little rebarred hole on the side and shined the flashlight in. Nothing. We saw nothing. The light just wasn't strong enough. It just shone off into infinity. We climbed up to the top and tried again with the same results.

"Stupid flashlight! We just wasted all our money!" I began to cry.

"Nuh, uh!" she protested. "We're like scientists. We just discovered something amazing. It just means the pit is very, very deep, maybe even bottomless."

"You mean if you fell in there you'd just keep falling?" I asked, thinking about flinging the flashlight down along with my sister. I whipped a stone down instead. We heard a little clunk. A few more stones produced consistent results.

"Or maybe it's like another dimension in there, where the light can't shine," Barbara added quickly.

"Sure, OK, but let's go swimming. I'm really hot. Maybe we can get back in time to jump off the diving board for the Polaris." We talked not at all on the way back. That night in my bed I cried as I thought about the giant teddy bear at Schultz Brothers.

Barbara was up long before me the next morning, and when I finally came down the stairs I was met by a smiling Barbara, who swiftly moved me out onto the porch out of my mom's hearing range. "I found it! I found the entrance!"

I was angry that she'd explored it without me and jealous, as I'd hoped to be the hero who would find it. Still, I was excited. "So, what's inside?"

"I didn't get in. I couldn't open it. I need your help."

I loved being needed, and with that I eagerly got dressed and carried the heavy flashlight all the way back to the cave. The trip went more quickly as we continued wearing down a path. We found the little rebarred hole and then climbed up over the top. Across the other side, and on down the little hill there were two rusty doors lying on the ground. "It's a tornado shelter!" I yelled. These doors are just like Dorothy's, remember when she tried to get in but they didn't hear her? I I bet this is a tornado shelter, probably for that farm house we saw over there!"

She laughed. "Do you think this is Kansas or something? There's no tornadoes here. Come on, help me pull." I set the flashlight down carefully and got a good grip on the metal door. We both pulled as hard as we could. We counted to three and pulled in unison. We prayed for help. We tugged some more. We found some large sticks and tried to pry them open, but the doors wouldn't budge. We returned home, hot and discouraged.

At dinner time I asked my mom if there were ever tornadoes in Wisconsin. She said there could be, but it didn't happen very often. I cast a smug "Told you so" look at Barbara, who cast back a "Don't you dare talk about this in front of Mom" kind of look. Our secret had been safe so far. The intense heat spell finally broke that evening. Dark clouds gathered, and the trees began to sway wildly. I asked my mom where we'd go if there was a tornado, since we had no basement. "Don't worry, this is only a thunderstorm. I just hope the power doesn't go out." She and Barbara were absorbed in an old cowboy movie. I stepped onto the porch and watched leaves and sticks flying off the trees. My mom's nonchalance about the storm, together with the fact that we had no tornado shelter, suddenly had me terrified. We should have been running to the shelter at that very moment, but there probably wasn't time anyway. It was getting darker by the minute. Even if we could get there before the tornado, I wasn't convinced that we could pry open the doors, even with my mom's help. I wished my dad were there, for surely he could open the doors, but he wouldn't be up until Friday night. Huge raindrops began falling and thunder shook the whole house. I went back inside and sat on the couch beside Barbara. The lights blinked a few times and then went off, along with the TV. Serves them right, I thought. My mother fumbled in the drawer where we kept the flashlights and tried a few of them. "I guess all the batteries must be dead," she said.

"Oh, it's OK, we've got a . . ."

"Candle," Barbara shouted as she jabbed me in the ribs. Our flashlight had been safely hidden from my mother who was to know nothing of our cave exploration. I'd almost blown it after crossing my heart and everything. My mom finally lit a candle, and prattled on about how cozy it was. Barbara agreed. I sat silently on the couch, trying to hide the fact that I shuddered with every flash of lightening and every clap of thunder. The storm abated quickly enough, but we'd been in bed for a long time before the power came back on. I laid in the dark scared and creeped out, imagining what kinds of slimy things we'd have encountered if we'd made it to the tornado shelter.

A few days passed without any thoughts or actions on the cave. My dad came up on Friday night bringing steaks and watermelon and promises of boat rides and fun. He always watched the 10 o'clock news, and being his first night and all, we were allowed to stay up with him until it was over. I was coloring a picture, hearing only partially and understanding not at all. Barbara on the other hand, was listening as carefully as she was able. After we were in bed she whispered to me, "I don't think the cave is a root cellar or a tornado shelter. I think it was built as a bomb shelter during World War II. The people up here were afraid of being bombed by Hitler because they were hiding Jews. In fact, they probably hid them down inside of there." We'd seen plenty of scary war movies where everyone was running for bomb shelters, and adults talked about the war occasionally.

"Well, I'm sure glad we don't have to run from those bombs. Maybe there's tunnels and secret rooms and stuff down there where they hid people. Do you think?"

"There could be, but it's probably *still* a bomb shelter. You know the Russians are getting ready to bomb us. Everyone at school was talking about it before we got out, and I heard something about it on TV tonight."

"Dad said that wasn't what they meant. I heard him."

"Well, of course he's gonna say that so we don't worry, but that's the truth. We're pretty lucky to have that bomb shelter there, actually."

I thought about my girlfriend in the city. They had a bomb shelter in their house stocked with food and water. "But there's no food there, and you can't even get inside, and it might not even have a bottom or it might be a different, dim, duh, what did you call it?" This was a terror worse than the tornado. I waited to hear some answers from Barbara, but all I heard was her gentle regular breathing. "Barbara, Barbara! Are you asleep?" She obviously was, or was faking it, leaving me to wrestle my fears alone. I listened for airplanes. Every time I heard a boat motor in the night I was sure it was a Russian plane on its way. I don't know how long I lay awake worrying, but it was long after my parents' light was off, and long after the crickets had stopped singing for the night.

The following week Barbara's friend Judy came up to stay for a few days. Barbara had plenty of normal friends; I couldn't imagine why she'd invited Judy the Genius up to the lake. I mean, sitting on the snow banks at recess studying spelling words in February was one thing, but to spend time with a studious prude in Lake Geneva in July was absurd. It must have been my parents' idea. They admired her seriousness, maturity and intelligence. They figured she was a good influence on my sister. Judy had blown in from Boston sometime in the middle of her third grade year, upsetting the status quo by winning the school spelling bee. This simply had never been done before. Most third graders didn't even try. The name, "Judy the Genius," had been created by a jealous sixth grader, and was adopted immediately by the whole school, even by us little kids. The name just fit so well with the funny way she talked and with her long nose and pointy glasses. In fourth grade she got to go all the way to Springfield for the state spelling competition. Naturally she was every teacher's pet. I couldn't imagine what she and Barbara were going to do all week. I pictured Judy studying over the Wall Street Journal, discussing the stock market with my dad on Friday night.

She hadn't been with us five minutes before Barbara had shared with her every secret detail we'd discovered about the cave. I couldn't believe it. What betrayal! When I managed to get Barbara alone for a minute I laid into her for breaking our secret pact. Barbara was quick to point out that I was the one who'd crossed my heart and hoped to die if I ever told anyone. She'd made no such promise. Besides that, with Judy's help we might be able to get the doors open and, Judy, being the smartest kid at Jefferson

Elementary School just might be able to solve the mystery for us. I didn't believe Prudy Judy's skinny little arms and oversized brain were capable of any such thing.

Judy's brain kicked into overdrive. She immediately dismissed the root cellar/tornado shelter theory due to the fact that the farmhouse was too far away. I suspect it was just too dull and boring for her imagination, but I didn't know that then. She was more excited about our other ideas, but had to create a few of her own. "From what you're describing, I believe it's an old Indian burial ground, or maybe even a fort. We need to inspect the grounds for old pottery shards and arrowheads." Her confidence was contagious; she won me over. We knew she'd figure it out once she saw it. Off we went, the three of us, flashlight in tow, up the hill, through the field, past the apple trees and the wild raspberries, and into the thick mosquito infested woods.

"Maybe it was part of the underground railroad. I know Wisconsin played a big part in that movement." Judy said. I thought immediately about the subway in Chicago.

"What was that?" I asked. After Judy tried to explain, I still pictured the Chicago subway, but with escaped slaves riding on trains. Surely, if it were so, we'd find the tracks down there.

We made our way immediately to the doors. The three of us gripped hard, counted to three and pulled with all our might. It moved. It was only a few inches, but the rusty metal door had slid sideways. The hinges were rusted and totally broken off. We repeated the action again and again until we had an opening of about two feet. Eagerly we looked down, anticipating a stairway or some deep dark tunnel, but all we found were some old pipes and a big old faucet handle. The doors covered a rectangle about twelve inches deep. We poked around with a stick hoping to find an opening, but it was solid ground. This obviously was not the entrance. This had nothing at all to do with the cave. Greatly disappointed, we headed toward the top, searching for pottery and arrowheads on the way. We reached the hole and once again attempted to shine the flashlight down. We yelled into it, spat down it, and threw rocks. We repeated all of this from the little rebarred hole on the side, and smelled the musty odor. We waited for Judy to come up with a verdict. "It kind of smells like something dead and decaying; leaves, or animals, or . . ." She raised her eyebrows and looked at both of us, allowing us to imagine the worst.

"Let's go home," I suggested. For once, Barbara agreed.

Judy said, "We've probably done all the investigating we can do anyway with what we've got. When we get back we need to record our findings and approach this mystery in a scientific manner." Arriving back home we pulled out pencil and paper and Judy began meticulously describing what we'd seen. "Did you measure those holes yet?" she asked. I couldn't quite see the point but said nothing so as not to expose my ignorance. On the following sheet of paper we began listing all of our theories, beginning with the dull boring ones, like garbage dump and root cellar.

"Why don't we ask Ian what it is?' I suggested.

"Is that the guy that cuts your lawn?"

"Uh-huh."

How would he know? He's just a caretaker."

"He's lived around here his whole life and his family has a root cellar."

"You idiot!" Barbara interjected, "We can't tell anybody about this. Anyway, he never goes back there into those woods. In fact, nobody has been back there for, gosh, I don't know, twenty or thirty, or maybe a hundred years."

We continued making the list: grain storage, slave hideout, bomb shelter, Jewish hideout, cowboy fort, Indian fort, Indian burial ground, witch gathering place, tomb . . .

"Tomb? You mean a place where a dead person is buried?" I asked.

"Yes, like in ancient Egypt! The pharaohs were embalmed and buried in tombs along with provisions to take to the next world. Like lots of gold and stuff." It turned out that Judy was some sort of expert on all this being that her older sister had studied ancient Egypt in the sixth grade, and Judy herself had seen a museum exhibit when she visited New York City.

"A tomb?" Barbara asked. "A TOMB!" Barbara yelled. This information sat very well with all three of us. Before jumping to conclusions, however, we decided that we needed to learn more on the subject.

Once again we made an emergency walk into town, this time to visit the library. I didn't expect Judy could walk all that way, but the lure of the library gave her the strength and energy. As we walked past the mansions we prided ourselves on being able to repeat back to Judy many of the facts we'd heard when we rode the sightseeing boat home. She loved the Morton Salt house best and longed to "have tea on the terrace and converse with the owners."

The lady at the library showed us where to find the *World Book Encyclopedia*, and pulled some books off the shelf on ancient Egypt and King Tut's tomb. The reading was too difficult for me, but I enjoyed looking at the pictures. I grew hungry and bored long before Judy and Barbara did, but being on the verge of great discovery, I didn't complain. I stared out at the lake, watching the boats go by. After what seemed like hours, the older girls were totally stoked by what they'd read and ready to carry on the mission. We left the library, and walked downtown discussing our bright future. Nobody in the whole world, except for us, knew the whereabouts of that tomb. Judy promised that someday our names would be "immortalized" in books at the library. Sightseeing boats would glide past our cottage and tell all the tourists about our brilliant discovery. Kids at school would be totally envious. We probably couldn't go to restaurants and public places anymore because everyone would want our autographs. Better than the fame, however, would be the fortune. We walked past Arnold's drugs and Barbara talked about all the movie magazines she'd be able to buy. I drooled in front of Bittner's Bakery, knowing that the next time I was in town I'd be able to buy anything and everything I wanted there. Passing the windows of the Smart Shop and Bartons, Judy picked out clothes for her mom, her sister and herself. Finally we got to Schultz Brothers where I smiled up at my teddy bear, still in the window. "Oh, what a cute bear!" Judy said. "I'm gonna ask my mom to buy it for me when she picks me up on Sunday."

"But that's my bear," I shouted, "and I'm gonna buy him just as soon as we get our money!"

Judy smiled down at me. "Well, we'll see."

Barbara distracted us when she suddenly yelled, "I'm gonna buy that T bird!" as a hot red convertible glided past us.

"I'd prefer an Austin Healey, but you won't see any in this town," Judy exclaimed.

"I want a Rambler station wagon, just like Mom's friend Helen has," I said. They laughed.

"That's a cheap junky car; you don't want one of those!" Judy explained.

We walked through the Riviera where the smells teased our appetites mercilessly. We had no money but were content, knowing that this would be the last time we would find ourselves here, hungry and broke. From there we started back on the shore path. When we passed the Wrigley's place Judy claimed their beautiful boat, the Ada E. Barbara quickly claimed the Normandy from across the lake. They decided they would race them up and down the lake from Fontana to Lake Geneva.

"I'll be docking my boat at the Morton Salt mansion, which I will buy," Judy announced, for surely there was enough gold down there for all that. I figured I'd better get my bid in quickly, and said I'd buy the house on Black Point.

"That scary old thing!" Barbara said. "I'm gonna buy Flowerside Farm, together with the lake mansion. We'll be neighbors, Judy! I'm gonna raise horses. You can buy Green Gables farm; we'll breed world famous Arabians."

"But I love Green Gables. What farm do I get to buy?"

"You'll be way on the other side of the lake," Barbara observed. "You wouldn't be able to get all the way over here every day to feed your horses. I'm sure they got lots of farms over there as well." I was feeling banished. The conversation moved into travel destinations, places they'd studied about last year in school. Then they discussed jewels, diamonds and emeralds that I knew nothing about and cared about even less. These they would find directly in the cave, or purchase with their portion of the money. They planned on wearing them on their yacht parties, to which only kids in their grade would be invited. As we passed the wooded lot beside our cottage, Judy decided she would also buy that and build a grand hotel there. It would be elegant, like the one she'd stayed at in New York City. There'd be doormen and room service. On the twentieth floor there'd be a grand dining room that would look out over the whole lake. There'd also be a big heated swimming pool and a huge pier where diners could pull up with their boats. Barbara didn't object. In fact, she seemed excited about it.

"But what about the baby foxes?" I asked. "Where are they supposed to go?"

Barbara answered, "There's plenty of woods around here where they can go. Anyway, we haven't seen them since last summer, they're probably long gone."

"But what about our fort?" I asked her.

She looked at me with disgust, "Aren't we a little big for forts?" Funny, she hadn't been too big when we built it two weeks earlier.

"You'll forget all about it when you see this place," Judy assured me. "I'll let you swim in the pool and eat in the restaurant and stuff. You'll be living across the lake by then and you can come by boat for dinner."

"Do you think there's enough room here for a giant hotel?" Barbara asked.

"The contractors will determine that. I might have to purchase the properties next to it as well."

"But they've all got cottages on them already," I protested.

"So, you demolish them. That's called progress."

"You wouldn't tear down our cottage, would you?"

"Believe me, when you see this place, and after you've moved into your mansion across the lake, you won't care one iota about your dinky cabin." Dinky cabin, my foot! I wanted to tell my mom just what this intelligent, mature and serious little prude was up to. I wanted my mom to know that Judy planned to destroy the woods and put up a huge hotel right over our house. Without telling her about the treasure, however, there'd be no way she'd take me seriously. She'd only laugh.

After we got home I cornered Barbara. "It's not fair that we've got to share the treasure with Judy. She didn't discover the cave. She doesn't even live here! She's gonna buy up everything around here and ruin it all! You've got to stop her!"

I expected a little support from the animal and nature lover. Instead she lay into me, "You are so selfish!!! Judy's my best friend. Why, without her, we wouldn't even know about the tomb. You thought it was a stupid tornado shelter. Besides, I discovered it, remember? Maybe it's you that shouldn't share the treasure!"

After that I went off by myself, down to our secret fort in the woods by the lake. I hoped to see the foxes, thinking their existence might convince Barbara not to let Judy share our fortune. I almost wished we'd never discovered the stupid cave, or tomb, or whatever it was, and I especially wished Judy had never come. When I got back to the house, their speculations on how to spend the fortune had been replaced by more practical concerns. They were trying to figure out how to tell the world about the discovery and yet keep thieves away. Besides, we still had to get in and figure out a way to haul out all of the treasure. Nothing was resolved that night, but Judy suggested we sleep on it.

By the time I got up the next morning, it had already been decided. As soon as my mother left, we would take the ropes off both ends of the speedboat. We'd tie them together and drag them up to the cave. (We ended up taking the ski rope as well, not knowing exactly how deep the cave was.) We'd tie the rope around my waist and lower me down from the hole on top, flashlight in tow. It had to be me, as I was the smallest, lightest and weakest. I was to look for the treasure and tie pieces onto the rope. They'd haul it up, one piece at a time. Eventually they'd haul me back up too. My protestations were met with accusations of not doing my part, threats of not being able to share the treasure, and insults about being a scaredy cat. After all that, I was cajoled into believing that I was especially talented for this job due to my sensitive fingers, and my perfect size for slipping through the hole. I'd be the first human to actually see the treasure since before the time of Christ. That would make me especially famous. I was doing the world of archaeology a big favor. Barbara and Judy would love me forever, and besides all that, I'd get to buy the teddy bear from Schultz Brothers.

The hike back up to the cave went way too quickly. We found ourselves back on top standing before the hole. It was definitely wide enough for me to fit through. "Now, whatever you do," Barbara said, "Don't drop the flashlight."

"Let me show you," Judy offered graciously. "Right hand here on the top, left hand here down below, and hold it tight and close to your body. That way you've got three points of contact and are much less likely to drop it." I froze in position, gripping the flashlight against my body as though my life depended on it. They tied a big loop in the rope and asked me to step into it. My curiosity about the cave suddenly vanished and in a flash, right then and there, I decided to throw away fame, fortune and the approval of Judy and my sister. As I was trying to decide whether to vocally protest or just run, we were distracted by a rustling noise in the woods; something was coming up the hill and right for us. Before we had time to react, a short, squat, old woman with a mean, wrinkly face popped out of the woods. "You kids get away from this old cistern!!" she screamed.

"This what?" Judy asked.

"You heard me you little trespassing brats, scram! This is private property, scram before I call the sheriff."

I was scramming all right. The flashlight got dropped somewhere, never to be seen again, at least not by us. I darted through the woods along the worn path. I didn't stop when I got to the orchard. I was out of breath, my side ached, but I kept scramming. I nearly flew down the hill to the house and slammed the door behind me. I grabbed a bottle of root beer and hid in the closet.

After a long while I heard laughter. It was Judy and Barbara coming down the hill. I was relieved, and left my place of safety. They sauntered through the door all hunched over, imitating the old lady. "Get away from that old cistern!" they screeched in a witchy sounding voice.

"What's a cistern?" I hollered, above their laughter.

"It's like a tank, a tank to hold water."

"You mean, that's all it is? It's just a stupid old water tank?"

"I knew it all along," Judy said. Barbara agreed.

4

Cousin Debbie

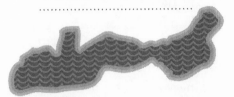

Summer, blissful summer, had finally arrived. We were up at the lake to stay. Ten weeks of freedom stretched before us; freedom to be outdoors, hiking along the lake path, exploring the woods, building forts, climbing trees, rolling down our steep grassy hill and swimming for hours and hours in the cool, clear lake. My demanding teacher and all the creeps from my fourth grade class were safely back in Chicago and out of my life. We were eating supper out on the porch when the phone rang. Five minutes later Mom came back effervescing with joy. "Guess what? I've got great news!" Her attitude filled us with excitement and eager anticipation.

"What?"

"Aunt Mary and your cousin Debbie are coming tomorrow. Debbie's going to stay with us for a whole week! Isn't that just the best?" Why couldn't it have been something a little easier to take, like, "It's time for polio shots," or "Somebody died."

"Oh," I responded flatly, trying not to let out my true feelings.

Barbara, however, on the edge of puberty, didn't hold back. "A week? Seven whole days with that little twerp? Does she have to come?"

"Barbara! What kind of rotten attitude is that? You ought to be ashamed of yourself! I certainly am! Anyway, she's coming mostly to play with Sandy. But I'm warning you," she spoke sternly shaking her forefinger at Barbara, "You'd better be nice to her." Being nice to Debbie entailed playing all the stupid little games she wanted to play, and pretending to like it. Barbara refused, had always refused, sticking me with the task. Sadly, I was really good at it. So good, in fact, that my mother had no clue about my true feelings toward Debbie. Unwittingly I'd become the good kid, the one Mom could count on to be nice, compliant, agreeable and hospitable. She smiled at me, "You're going to have so much fun."

Debbie really didn't deserve all the hatred we felt for her. She really liked me back then. It wasn't her fault that she was an only child and spoiled rotten. It was partly the attitudes of the adults that created our loathing. Aunt Mary had tried for six years to have her, so when she finally came, she was adored and heavily doted upon. My mom had known my dad only six weeks when she succeeded at getting pregnant. I followed easily, three years later, so we were adored a lot less and doted upon not at all. From the time of her birth there had been some sort of unwritten agreement that all people needed to dote upon fragile little Debbie who took so long to be born. Aunt Mary was the kind of woman no one dared defy. I was three years older than Debbie, so I was expected to appease her, give in, let her have her way. She was an indoor kid who loved TV and games. During a dark Chicago winter, when it was twenty below zero, or pouring rain, I could tolerate staying indoors and playing stupid games with her; but I didn't want to waste a single minute of my short summer.

Up in our bedroom that night I asked Barbara through my tears, "Barbara, what am I going to do?"

"Do? Oh don't worry, we'll think of lots of good things!" Her mischievous, malevolent smile was reassuring.

The few hours we had before her arrival the next day were spent devising ways to torment Debbie. We tried to make a booby trap, digging a hole and filling it with water. Then we covered it with a thin cloth and covered that with a very thin layer of dirt, hoping she'd step on it and fall into the muddy water. We stared out into the woods and concocted wild stories about poisonous spiders, boa constrictors, vicious dogs, hungry bears and psychopathic vagabonds. We poured over every detail in order to get our stories synchronized. We'd scare her so badly she'd beg to go home early. We noted where the nettle and the poison ivy grew, hoping to lead her into both. This planning frenzy proved to be cathartic, but little else.

When their car drove down our steep driveway I felt like someone had stabbed me, right through the heart. Debbie came bounding out of the car, "We're here. We're here! Sandy, we're here!" No kidding! She was dressed in yellow shorts with a matching polka dot shirt with little lace-lined pockets. Shopping for Debbie was one of Aunt Mary's chief obsessions. Debbie's perfect little braids were decked out in yellow ribbons. She wore huge glasses that made her look rather like a bug, a giant cockroach that I wanted to smash.

Debbie's behemoth mother emerged slowly out of the car. She stood tall and firm analyzing the cottage from top to bottom. Then she became aware of us, smiled, and said, "So nice to see you girls. Debbie has so many surprises for you. We brought lots of games; Sorry, Chutes and Ladders, Chinese checkers and several more. I didn't know which ones you had up here." Then she pointed up at the eaves, "Be sure to tell your father to remove those wasp nests up there. I don't want Debbie to get stung."

Mom and Aunt Mary embraced; then Mom reached down and gave Debbie a huge hug. Gosh, the only time she had ever hugged me like that was after she thought I'd been kidnapped. "Oh, Debbie, don't you look cute. I'm so glad you're going to get to stay with us." We were ordered to help drag Debbie's two

suitcases and multiple hand bags up to our small bedroom, which had already been reduced in size by the
rollaway bed. She had at least one prissy perfect short
set for each day and all the latest in child's beachwear.
She was also prepared for bad weather, just in case. I
think it could've snowed and she'd have been alright.

As soon as all her stuff was crammed into our
room, she pulled out her Barbie doll and Barbie's
latest swimsuit with accessories. "Look I just got this.
We can bring her down to the lake, though we can't
actually put her in the water." I no longer played with
dolls, and I particularly hated Barbie. I wish I had
just told Debbie this, but, somehow, when it came to
Debbie, saying "no" was not an option.

"Maybe later," I replied.

It was really hot. It was the kind of day when you could stay in the water for hours on end and never feel cold. Everyone trooped down to the pier, but Barbara and I raced ahead and dove into the cold refreshing lake. Soon I was called into the shallow water to be with Debbie. Debbie did not know how to swim, and was, in fact, terrified of the water. "It's freezing," she cried, as we tried to coax her in with her life jacket on. "What's all that creepy green stuff down there?" With my mom at her side, Debbie managed to paddle around for about two minutes before turning blue. She was praised to the hilt. Then Aunt Mary wrapped her in a huge, newly purchased beach towel and hurried her up to the house to put on a dry bathing suit.

I challenged Barbara to a swimming race, and afterward continued to perfect my crawl, back and forth between our pier and the neighbor's, trying to keep in shape for the swim team. From our old wooden diving board I executed several forward somersaults in pike position, landing straight as an arrow, with hardly a splash. I was finally getting it. I hoped someone would notice, but no one did until I messed one up, landing flat on my back. By that time Aunt Mary and Debbie had returned. Aunt Mary walked to the edge of the pier, "You're going to get hurt. I think you've had enough swimming." As if the slap on the back hadn't been punishment enough!

I looked at Mom to rescue me, "She's right Sandy, come out now and play with Debbie. She's waiting for you." We spent the rest of the day on the lawn dressing Barbie.

I thought my aunt would never leave that evening. She had never left Debbie for such a long time before. I hoped and prayed she'd change her mind. I overheard Aunt Mary share with my mother, "They say that children need some separation from us for healthy development. I know this week is going to be good for Debbie. I'm not ready to send her off to Girl Scout camp yet, you hear such awful things." Sandy and I were confident that we could outdo the Girl Scouts. Aunt Mary was eight years older than Mom and had served as a surrogate mother as my grandmother had suffered frequent bouts of illness when they were young. She held sway over Mom that real parents could only dream of. Aunt Mary left Mom with a carefully typed list of instructions for Debbie's care and maintenance, including before bedtime rituals and sleep requirements, dietary requirements, restrictions and preferences, and forbidden TV shows and entertainment.

"Don't worry!" Mom finally told her. "We'll take good care of her." My mom was sincere.

Before bed that night we suffered through Debbie's agonizing decision over which pair of new baby doll pajamas to wear first, and how to fit each of her stuffed animals onto the hard narrow rolla-way bed. Debbie was accustomed to her own double canopy bed. "I can't sleep on this hard mattress," she complained.

"You're going to have to," Barbara told her, "it's the only extra bed we've got. Now I'm tired. Go to sleep!"

A few minutes later Debbie perked up again, "Sandy, can I sleep with you?"

"Debbie, my bed isn't big enough."

"But I can't sleep."

Barbara screamed at her, "Shut up! Just go to sleep before I smack you." Debbie flew out of bed and went racing to my mother's room. Soon the two came back together, my mother wiping Debbie's tears away. She tucked her neatly into bed, my bed, with all her little animals, while I was sent to sleep on the rollaway bed.

Barbara and I were eager to get started on all of our pranks, but dreaming them up had been much easier than actually initiating them. We managed to slip in a few scary suggestions about the poisonous and ferocious woodland creatures, which firmed up Debbie's resolve to play indoors. My mom, for the most part, wasn't letting any of us out of her sight. It was not like my mother to be so attentive. Perhaps she was on to us. "Mom, aren't you going golfing today?" She always golfed on Wednesdays.

"No, not today. We're going to teach Debbie how to swim." As many minutes as Debbie could tolerate the cold water, my mother was working with her. Debbie made up a stupid song. "Kick, paddle, paddle, paddle, kick, paddle paddle, paddle . . ." I heard this chanted all week long, in and out of the water. It wasn't enough that my mother was fully devoted to this task, but I, too, was commandeered into standing in the shallow water, watching and praising Debbie's feeble efforts. I longed to be racing and diving with Barbara, though on most days she managed to disappear.

Due to her fair skin, Debbie was to have only limited amounts of sunlight. When her time ran out, I was doomed to sit on the screen porch with her, playing board games or Barbie. She couldn't stand to lose a game. Once she realized she was losing, her face would get all tight, tears would well up inside, and then she'd take drastic measures. Once she actually dumped over the Chinese checker board, pretending it was an accident when I got too far ahead of her. On spinner games she'd stick out her baby finger to stop it exactly where she wanted it to be. Similarly, if dice were involved, she would keep re-rolling until she got something she liked. One afternoon Barbara emerged onto the porch and caught Debbie pilfering funds from the Monopoly bank. "Hey, you're cheating! You can't do that!"

"Barbara, leave those girls alone!" Mom shouted from the kitchen.

I could've cared less. My heart was out in the woods where I should have been romping and exploring. A few times, late in the afternoon, when the sun was no longer strong, I suggested, "Hey, why don't we take a little walk along the lake path?"

"Why?"

"Well, because, it's nice. It's fun. You get to walk along the water and see lots of cool things."

"No, I hate to walk. I want to play."

"Ok, let's go outside. We can roll down the hill. It's really fun."

"Oh, no, the grass will make me itch."

Barbara insisted I was being way too nice to her. "You don't have to do everything she wants. Just go off and if she wants to stay back with Mom, just let her." Barbara was right. I guess I could've done that, but then I knew my mom would be angry with me. "You certainly don't have to let her cheat! I can't believe you let her get away with that stuff. Maybe you deserve to be stuck with her." Deserve? Now I was confused. Being good, compliant and agreeable were the few virtues I had going for me, but now Barbara was telling me I was being punished for it. It was time to do something. I mustered up my courage, and when we were out of Mom's earshot, I began to tell Debbie a few of the scary stories we'd concocted. She cast a nervous glance toward the woods, but was otherwise unmoved by my creativity. I stuck a crayfish in her aqua blue tennis shoe, the one that matched the aqua blue beach robe, but it must have crawled out before she put it on. I stuck poison ivy in her bed, well, my bed actually. She never caught it, but I did. I put some daddy long leg spiders on the table just before dinner, but these were smashed by my mother before we could get so much as a wince out of Debbie; poor spiders. The cayenne pepper I sprinkled onto her portion of shepherds' pie earned her extra ice cream. If only I'd gotten caught at these pranks, things might have been alright. Despite all my valiant efforts, Debbie still adored me, and Mom still thought I was her good, obedient daughter. I was a total failure. I was not lovable and adorable like Debbie apparently was, but I couldn't succeed at being bad either.

When the neighbor stopped by one afternoon, my mother made a special effort to introduce her beloved niece. "This," she said, obviously bursting with pride, "is my niece, Debbie. Debbie, this is our neighbor, Mrs. Murphy."

Debbie extended her chubby little hand, 'Pleased to meet you, Mrs. Murphy."

"Isn't she a darling? And so polite. My sister has done a superb job raising her."

Barbara whispered to me, "In contrast to some other mother we all know."

That night my mother fixed her famous hot dog casserole. Debbie looked up at my mother like a poor lost pound puppy, and with tears in her eyes, she confessed, "I'm so sorry, Auntie Irma, but I don't like this." My mother looked crestfallen.

"Oh, Debbie, I'm sorry. Barbara and Sandy love it."

"No we don't!" Barbara piped in.

My mother cast an angry disgusted look at Barbara and then asked Debbie if she'd like some macaroni and cheese instead.

"Oh, can we have some?" I asked, hopefully.

"Don't *you* start in! Just eat the casserole!"

Every night after dinner it was, "Thank-you for dinner, Auntie Irma. May I be excused, please?" and, "I love to dry dishes, Auntie Irma, may I help you?" Barbara and I were reaching the boiling point. Before bed it was, "Thank you for a wonderful day. Will you listen to my prayers, please, Auntie Irma?" The listening ritual was probably on Aunt Mary's care and maintenance instructions. My mother never forgot. "Thank-you, God, for my wonderful Auntie Irma and my cousins, Barbara and Sandy."

On Friday I woke up feeling a bit happier, knowing that my dad would be up that evening and he'd take us out on the boat. It was the height of the week for me. Debbie was also excited that it was Friday. "Oh, today is Friday. *Swiss Family Robinson* is going to be on *Family Classics* tonight. It's one of my favorite movies."

"But Debbie, we probably won't watch it. My dad comes tonight. If he gets here early enough he'll take us out on the boat!" Debbie looked devastated.

It was a perfect night for a sunset cruise. My dad had gotten there in plenty of time, dinner was out of the way and we were ready. Standing on the pier, ready to climb in the boat, Debbie suddenly began complaining to my mom. "Oh, Auntie Irma, my stomach. My stomach hurts badly."

"Did you eat too much? Something we ate for dinner?"

"I don't know, but I feel like I'm going to throw up."

"Ooooooh gross!" said Barbara. My dad looked alarmed.

Debbie continued, holding her stomach all the while, "I'm afraid the rocking in the boat will make me sick." My mother felt her forehead and then walked her up to the house. She set her up on the couch with pillows and a blanket and a bucket, just in case.

I was already sitting in the boat, ready to go, but my mom yelled for me to come back up to the house. I climbed up the hill reluctantly, and was met by my smiling mother, "Honey, I need you to stay here with Debbie. We found a wonderful movie that you two can watch. We'll be back before it's over."

By Sunday evening Debbie had finally pushed me over the edge. My dad had already left to go back to the city. The weekend had come and gone. Barbara had spent the entire weekend helping my dad work on the boat. I'd not gotten a single boat ride, but had managed no less than six games of Monopoly, six of Sorry, multiple hands of War, at least eight of Candy Land and four of Chutes and Ladders. I also got to watch Barbie get married five or six times. Mom was preparing dinner and Debbie and I were on the porch playing Crazy Eights. I was gazing longingly down at the lake, which was now smooth as glass and painted by the setting sun, perfect for swimming. Debbie smiled at me and said, "Sandy, you're not only my cousin but my very best friend too!" I hated her guts. How had I so totally and completely failed to convey this to her? I could imagine, even then, that someone like Debbie might have difficulty making friends, but I felt no sympathy. I heard no compliment. My sense of failure was acute and my anger fierce.

At that moment Barbara suddenly shouted, "Hey, look, a turtle down in the lake!" A turtle sighting always required a run down the hill for a closer look. I couldn't tell if it was a turtle or a piece of flotsam. It didn't matter. It was a joyful diversion, like a fire drill at school. I darted from the table, and out the screen door.

"I don't have my shoes on!" screamed Debbie.

"Come anyway. The turtle won't stay there forever. Just come on." I didn't wait. Barbara and I tore down the hill and tiptoed carefully out on the pier hoping not to scare the turtle. We watched its little head above the water's surface. Debbie was slowly and fearfully picking her way down the grassy hill. We glanced at her, rolled our eyes, and focused back on the turtle.

We, and the turtle, were startled by Debbie's yell from the edge of the pier, "I don't have my life jacket." The turtle quickly submerged.

"You scared him!" shouted Barbara. I leaned over and tried to see him under the water, hoping he'd swim into the shadow of the pier.

Again Debbie yelled, "I don't have my life jacket."

"So what!" I yelled back.

Debbie came tiptoeing out, "I'm sorry. I so wanted to see him."

I stood up. "Well, he's down there somewhere. He's got to come up for air eventually."

Debbie leaned over cautiously, taking my place on the edge of the pier. "Here turtly, turtly, turtly. Here turtly, turtly . . . ." Her babyish chatter was obnoxious, and everyone knows you don't call a turtle! The turtle surely wouldn't surface now. Suddenly my frustration got the best of me, and Debbie's vulnerable position was irresistible. I gave her a big shove. She toppled right over into the lake, letting out a little scream as she went. Quickly I became aware of what it meant not to be able to swim. She sank slowly to the bottom, evidently forgetting the "Kick, paddle, paddle," she'd rehearsed orally all week long. Her glasses had flown off so I could see her big, buggy eyes, huge and white, staring up at me. The little red bows on her pigtails were the last thing in my view. It was horrid. I hadn't meant to drown her. What had I meant to do? I was just angry. Right, tell it to the judge! Weird thoughts flashed through my mind. I wondered how they'd transport the body back to Chicago. I envisioned the funeral; my grandparents crying, Aunt Mary hysterical, and me absent, because I'd be in jail. I'd not only miss the next nine weeks of summer, but likely my entire childhood. I wondered if Aunt Mary would retrieve Debbie's Barbie doll and all her new clothes, or if my mom would just give them to the Salvation Army for the poor kids. Some poor kid was going to be mighty happy. We only gave them our junky old stuff.

Fortunately Barbara was quick and the lake was only about seven feet deep. She dove in and pushed Debbie up from underneath. I reached down and grabbed her hand. We managed to drag her over to the ladder just as my mom arrived. Once we got her up onto the pier, she coughed and sputtered a few times, then started screaming and crying. She vomited once or twice, but she was breathing and all.

I did not go to jail. The only words of reprimand I got were from Barbara. After Mom carried the crying Debbie up the hill, Barbara exclaimed angrily, "Are you nuts? You could have killed her. My god, Sandy, you're a *murderer*! But Barbara never told the real story. Debbie didn't either. I was unclear whether she really didn't know I'd pushed her, or if she simply couldn't believe I'd do such a thing and therefore dismissed it from her mind. Barbara became the hero of the day as Debbie went on and on how Barbara had saved her life. Aunt Mary was called, and together she and Debbie agreed that, due to her trauma, Debbie should go home a day early. I'd at least accomplished that much. I was relieved, though I was very nervous, not knowing when Debbie's memory might be jarred, or if Barbara might open her mouth. I was extra nice to Debbie that night and the next morning while we waited for her mother to arrive. We gleefully carried all her things down from the bedroom. As we were getting ready to say our long awaited good-byes, my mother looked at me and smiled, "Sandy we have a wonderful surprise for you. You get to go back to Chicago with Debbie and spend a week there."

"But, Mom, I ..."

"No 'ifs, ands or buts', it's been decided. I've already packed your things. Go on, now, Aunt Mary is waiting."

I knew I deserved it. If only I'd been caught! I don't know if my fear was distorting my perception, but as we were climbing into the car, Debbie looked at me slyly and said in a sinister voice, not her own, "Now *you* get to come to *my* house."

A Hug from Grandma

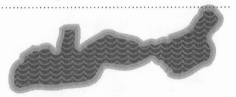

When I was very small, visits from Grandma and Grandpa were magical. They were huggy, kissy people, enveloped always in a cloud of laughter and joy. Their visits usually included a menagerie of aunts, uncles, cousins and friends, chicken, potato salad, Jell-O molds, cookies, donuts, kool-aid, and new toys. Grandma was adept at finding creative playthings, and Grandpa was equally adept at maximizing their full potential for fun. We had kites and sailboats and balls that we chased down the hill. Grandpa would run with us and roll in the grass. We'd play hide-and-seek and tag. I remember him swinging me like an airplane and hoisting me up on his broad shoulders so I could touch the leaves. I remember falling asleep in Grandma's warm embrace as Grandpa captivated the others with his glorious tenor voice and his amusing stories. Always, despite the crowds and chaos, they lavished me with affection and convinced me that I was the most precious being on earth. I was their little bunny rabbit, totally cute and totally loveable. So it was with eager anticipation that I stood on the platform of the Lake Geneva train station awaiting the arrival of my grandmother. She hadn't been up at the lake for two whole summers. There was the summer Grandpa had his operation, and then there was the summer Grandpa went to Heaven. The significance of this event was totally lost on my young mind. I had acted solemnly enough at the funeral, I knew it was expected, but I didn't understand what the big deal was. I envisioned him singing under a palm tree with a gentle ocean ebbing and flowing in the warm sunshine, waiting for the rest of us to join him. I resented the fact that Grandma had spent all of Christmas day in the bathroom crying, taking the jolly right out of my mother's carefully orchestrated Christmas. My mother had even less patience than I did for such behavior and we hadn't seen Grandma since, though Dad checked up on her regularly.

The warm platform was filled with people, but only Mom and I were there waiting for Grandma. Seeping through the thin walls of our cottage the night before, I'd heard her desperate plea, "What the heck am I supposed to do with your bitching, complaining mother for a whole week?" Despite Mom's insistence that picking up Grandma was Dad's responsibility, he was back in the city taking care of business. My older sister, Barbara, was at Girl Scout camp, an arrangement that had been made long before Grandma decided to come. I wore my new short set which showed off a bit of my midriff, and the white sandals Barbara had out grown. My hair had just been cut into a smart looking pixie. I knew Grandma would be impressed with how grown up I'd become.

An announcement came over a loud speaker that the train from Chicago was running ten minutes late. A few people groaned. A few moved into the shade of the depot. Mom lit another cigarette. Last time we were here Barbara and I had played tag up and down the brick platform and put pennies on the track. They were quite impressive after being run over by a loco-motive. But there were no kids to play with and no pennies, so I occupied my mind imagining the won-derful present Grandma would bring for me. I knew I couldn't possibly guess it, because it was always some-thing unusual and sensational. After what seemed like an hour I knelt down and stuck my ear on the track to listen for the train. An old lady with a funny hat yelled at me and then proceeded to lecture Mom on the dangers of a little girl putting her head on the railroad track. Although my mother allowed this to roll off her back, I was livid. Little Girl! Gosh I was nine and a half, and dressed like a teen-ager. After this I stood like a perfect little soldier beside my mother, consoling myself by imagining Grandma's warm loving embrace. I hadn't experienced it in far too long. Grandma would appreciate how grown up I looked, even if the lady with the funny hat hadn't. After what seemed like another hour we finally heard the distant train whistle. It sent waves of excitement and longing through me, for we had picked Grandma and Grandpa up here often when I was young. As the huge locomotive approached we could feel its powerful rumble. I strained unsuccessfully trying to see Grandma's face in the high dark windows.

Half of Chicago must have been on the train that day. People just kept pouring out the doors. The stream dried up to a trickle and then stopped. We waited a while longer and concluded that Grandma had somehow missed it. Just as we were about to give up, a porter popped through the door, lugging a couple of old familiar looking suitcases. Following him was Grandma, a little shorter, a little rounder and a little wearier than I'd remembered her, laden with shopping bags and boxes. I ran up to her and attempted to hug her, but it was awkward with all the stuff in her hands. She bent down and gave me a little peck of a kiss on the forehead. I wanted her to pick me up and swing me around, but I remembered that that had always been Grandpa's job. I was way too tall now anyway. I waited for her to tell me how much I'd grown and how cute I looked, but she was distracted by the porter and eager to get on with business. Between the porter, Grandma, Mom and me, we managed to haul all her stuff to our car. I slipped quietly into the back seat. Mom and Grandma made small talk in the front. "How was your trip?"

"The train was awfully crowded and hot. The tracks are really rough, especially around Crystal Lake, but it was OK, I guess."

"Well, how are you?" My mother immediately regretted asking.

"Well, you know. My arthritis is still bothering me. The blood pressure is still a little high, but the doctor doesn't want to change my medication. He said . . .," Mom's eyes caught mine in the rear view mirror. She rolled her eyes at me, summoning an ally for the difficult week ahead. Grandma continued, "He doesn't want to change the medication because it is helping some. Mostly it's just the loneliness. Nights are so difficult, I . . ."

"Well, never you mind," Mom cut her off. "Our beautiful sunsets and chirping crickets will take care of that. And the weather! Isn't it just exquisite?"

"Yes."

"Was it nice in Chicago, too?"

"A little too warm the last few days. It's nicer now, though we need rain." The conversation ran out after about three blocks. We sat in silence admiring the scenery along Snake Road.

As soon as we unloaded Grandma and all her stuff safely into the cottage, Mom made an announcement.

"I'm really sorry, but I have to run off. This is the week of the July tournament and I'm obligated to play golf every day."

"The July tournament," I piped in, "but that was . . ." Mom darted a glance my way that just about killed me, despite what they say. Some ally. "Help yourself to food. The refrigerator is full."

Grandma looked at me finally. "Well, it seems it's just you and me then. You've grown tall and skinny; I'm going to have to fatten you up while I'm here." Not exactly the compliment I'd been expecting. "What shall we do for lunch?"

Lunch? What about my gifts? I wanted to ask, but didn't. Surely all those sacks must have contained something for me. Let's fatten me up later. "I'm not really hungry yet, Grammy."

She sat on the porch staring out at the glistening lake. "It's as beautiful as I remember it." Her eyes began to fill with tears. I felt scared.

"Grammy," I quickly interrupted, "can I help you bring your packages upstairs?"

"Oh, the packages. That reminds me, I brought some things for you and Barbara." About time, Grandma!

"Oh, really?" I tried to sound surprised. As she handed me a beautifully wrapped shoe box, she was grinning widely, her eyes sparkling with the old kindness I had remembered. For just a fleeting moment I sensed the old adoration coming my way, as if her sole purpose in life was to please me. She stared on happily as I slowly and carefully opened the box. I wanted the moment to last. Out of the box I pulled a cheap baby doll complete with diapers and a bottle. Grandma didn't know I no longer played with dolls. I tried to hide my disappointment.

"I hope you're not too big for this," she said, "I just thought she was so cute. She so reminded me of you." I knew the insult wasn't intentional, but it hurt just the same. "Do you like her?"

"Oh, yes," I lied. I knew my liking the doll was imperative to Grandma's happiness. I was so afraid she'd start to cry if she knew how I really felt. "She's just beautiful, Grammy." I hugged the doll, the way Grandma had always hugged me, hoping she'd take the hint. She just stared at me until I broke the spell. "Grammy, we must come up with a name for her. Any ideas?"

"We'll think of something. But I've got more gifts." I was relieved. She wouldn't disappoint me again. She pulled out a bag full of ribbons, and then looked at me dumbfounded. "Your pigtails! Your beautiful pig-tails! Why ever did you cut them off?" She stared a moment longer. "Oh, never mind !" She shoved the ribbons back into her shopping bag and pulled out a large, flat box. "Here, here's something for you and Barbara to share." I opened it more quickly than the first, and discovered a set of plastic badminton rackets and plastic birdies, just like the ones they'd given us three years ago, the ones that didn't really work and were still sitting up in our closet.

"Oh," I exclaimed, "these look like so much fun! Barbara and I will really have fun with these. Hey, maybe you and I could play." I expected her to be flattered by my offer, though I was confident she'd reject it.

She smiled at me. "Wouldn't that be fun? But Grampy is the one who would have loved to play badminton with you. He was so athletic, so well-coordinated." She got quiet and I was afraid she was going to start to cry again.

"Maybe we should eat lunch," I had to distract her.

"Sure." My mother's idea of a full refrigerator meant two kinds of jelly to go along with the peanut butter and white bread. Grandma looked at it disdainfully, searched the cupboards, and then resigned herself. "I hope you don't eat like this every day for lunch," she said as she spread the peanut butter on the bread.

"No," I replied. Some days we just grabbed a few cookies, but I didn't tell her that. During lunch I struggled to think of things to say as we chewed. I didn't want Grandma to look at the lake and get sad again. "I love the doll Grammy. Maybe I'll call her Sally. Barbara will think she's really cute."

"What about your playhouse? The one Grampy built for you two. Do you still play in it?" Grandpa had built it lovingly and painstakingly out of scrap lumber and had allowed us to help him paint it. As young girls we'd spent hours playing in it, but we hadn't done so in recent years. It had fallen into disrepair and had become a storage shed for a great deal of junk and a home to a great variety of spiders. Dad meant to burn down the "eyesore," but hadn't gotten around to it. I'd have to be sure Grandma didn't get too close to it. "We still have it, Grammy. I can't wait to play with those badminton rackets. You know Barbara plays badminton in school. She's real good at it. Now she can practice. Too bad she isn't here now, or Mrs. Murphy's grandchildren. Anyhow, when they get back we're gonna have all kinds of fun." I sensed I was over doing it a bit. I took a big gulp of milk which Grandma insisted I drink in place of the coke I'd chosen.

"I'll definitely have to walk over and say 'hello' to Mrs. Murphy." Grandma seemed excited at this, her whole demeanor lightened a bit. She and Mrs. Murphy were around the same age and had always hit it off famously.

"That would be swell, Grammy, but they're not up here right now."

"Well, maybe on the weekend then." I didn't have the heart to tell her that Mrs. Murphy had suffered a stroke and probably wouldn't be up for the rest of the summer, if ever. The reality of that situation was hitting me for the first time, and I felt a sudden lump in my throat. Grandma looked at me inquisitively, "What's wrong dear?"

"Peanut butter. Caught in my throat."

"It figures. It's not very healthy you know. Drink some milk."

"Grammy, I can't wait to go swimming! Wait till you see how good I've gotten."

"Well, don't even think about it yet. You know very well you've just eaten and will get a severe cramp that will drown you. Let's clean up our lunch things." With that she walked into the kitchen and screamed, "Where did all these dishes come from? Does your mother always leave so many dishes around?"

"No, only sometimes." I was angry at my mom, but still felt the need to defend her. "This morning we had to pick you up at the train station. And she's playing in that big golf tournament so it's just been a really busy week for her."

Then Grandma got busy, and commandeered me into helping out. "Dear, you need to rinse those dishes more carefully. That soap will give you the trots." Some kind of déjà vu hit me with these words. Somebody, an older cousin, an aunt, or perhaps it had been my mom had been standing in my place, years before, and had received the same advice. Whoever it was had been foolish enough to argue, and I remember yelling and shouting that went on long after us kids had been sent to bed. So I rinsed them very very carefully, a slow and painstaking process.

Piles of dishes later, Grandma and I finally worked our way down to the lake. I'd been dying to get in the water all day. I was still hot from standing on the sunny platform. "You know, Grammy, I'm a much better swimmer than I was when you were last here. Last week Barbara and I swam all the way across the narrows while dad rowed." I hoped this would make her smile at me, but she continued to stare at the ground as we picked our way down the hill.

"Of course you're a good swimmer! You get it from Grampy. He used to swim competitively you know. Why if he'd had the chance, he could've competed in the Olympics. He was that good. Don't you remember how beautifully he used to swim? All the way to the point and back. In fact he taught you and Barbara how to swim. Don't you remember?"

I remembered Mom holding me in the water, day after day, showing me how to move my arms and legs, encouraging me to jump off the pier. No, I didn't remember Grandpa teaching me.

"Don't you remember?" she asked me again, a little impatiently.

"Sure, yes, of course." I lied.

I made no attempt to impress Grandma with my swimming. Olympic material I was not! At some point she told me I was turning my head way too far on the crawl. This, from a woman who couldn't even swim, was a little hard to take. I lay on my little blow up raft, put on my goggles and communed with the fish. Being with Grandma was beginning to tire me out. I stayed as long as I could, but soon my teeth began to chatter, so I had to climb out. I wanted Grandma to wrap me up in my big beach towel the way she used to and hug me till I got warm and dry. "Are you getting cold?" she asked, sounding surprised. "You need to keep moving in the water. You need to swim faster, then you won't get cold." I dried myself off and lay out in the sunshine closing my eyes.

"What is that?" she asked suddenly.

I opened my eyes, sat up and waved to the passengers on *The Lady of the Lake*. A few waved back. "That's the newest sightseeing boat. It was built by Gage Marine. It's modeled after a real steam boat, though it's not really a steam boat. It's called the *Lady of the Lake*, after a steam boat that was launched on this lake in 1873." I was proud of my knowledge, and longed for Grandma's words of approval and loving smile. She didn't look at me though. She just stared after the boat as it passed.

"I wish Grampy could've seen that, he'd have really liked it. We could have ridden on it."

"Maybe we still could, Grammy. You and me. They sell ice cream cones on board."

She looked at me sadly, "Oh, no, I don't think he'd like me going without him."

After that the sky began to cloud up. The hot sun couldn't manage to stay out for more than a few moments at a time, and I continued to shiver. So we made our way back up to the house. After changing my clothes I returned to the porch where Grandma was poking around in her bags. "I brought some-thing else for you," she said. Cookies, maybe, I hoped. Instead, she pulled out several old worn and tattered books. These books belonged to Dorothy, she loved them all. I thought it was time to pass them on."

"Dorothy?" I was puzzled. "Do I know her?"

"She would've been your aunt, but she died before you were born." Then it clicked. The Dorothy we were never, but never, under any circumstances, to mention in front of Grandma. The one cited as an example whenever we complained about polio shots. The one whose ghost Barbara used to imitate when she wanted to scare the living daylights out of me. I looked at the shabby books fearfully, wondering if they were conta-gious. Why had she brought them to me? Wouldn't the Salvation Army take them?

"What kinds of things do you like to read?" she asked.

"Well, um, it's summer, and I don't have any book reports due or anything. Um, well, I guess mostly I read Barbara's movie magazines."

"Your mother lets you read that trashy stuff?'

"Well, mostly I look at the pictures." I got a "You're pathetic" kind of look from Grandma.

"Here," she said as she handed me the first book. "*Heidi* was one of Dorothy's favorites." I was freaking out. Not only had she repeated the forbidden name but she placed the contaminated book right in my hands.

"I already saw the movie," I said defensively.

"Open it up," she said.

On the title page it said, "To Dorothy, Happy 10th birthday, Love Mommy and Daddy."

"Look through it," she urged. I paged through the enormous book. There were only a few pictures, and the Heidi wasn't nearly as cute as Shirley Temple. I didn't want Grandma to know it, but getting through a book of that type was for me a little like climbing Mount Everest.

I tried to remember my manners. "It's really nice, Grammy." Then she handed me several more classics equally thick and pictureless, including *Little Women, Pollyanna, Lassie Come Home, Rebecca of Sunny Brook Farm* and several others. "Did they all belong to, to ...," I couldn't get the forbidden name across my lips.

"Yes," she said firmly. "They all belonged to Dorothy. She loved them all and read them several times."

No wonder she died I thought rudely. "Shouldn't one of my older cousins get them?" I asked hopefully.

"No, sweet heart, I want you to have them." For a fleeting moment I caught that longed for glimmer of affection in her eyes. But she continued, "Now you've got plenty of good summer reading. Decide which one you want to start with, and we'll put the rest up on your bedroom shelf."

I was afraid of sleeping in the same room with the haunted books, but there was no arguing with Grandma. She looked inside the jacket of each one and reread Dorothy's name, then stroked each book as she carefully placed it on my shelf. She stared at me. Maybe she was waiting for a "thank-you," but I couldn't get one out. I just stood there. Her face began to tighten. She cast a last glance at the books and excused herself into the guest room.

Grandma remained hidden away for what seemed to be a very long time. I suspected she was crying. The shadows were beginning to lengthen across the front lawn meaning Mom could walk in anytime. I didn't want Mom to find her like that. I knew also that she would not appreciate Grandma's old junk accumulating in our little cottage. I paced the porch nervously imagining a show down between the two. I had to do something.

I walked back upstairs and knocked quietly on Grandma's door.

"Yes."

"Grammy, how'd you like to go for a walk along the lake?"

"Yes, dear. Yes, I'd like that very much. Just give me a few minutes. Wait downstairs. I'll be down quickly." While waiting I held the stupid baby doll up in the mirror and compared it to my face. I didn't see the resemblance.

Before we got out the door, Grandma looked down at my beautiful white sandals. Finally she had noticed them. I smiled, anticipating her compliments. "Don't you want to put on some better shoes? Those look so uncomfortable. You're going to get blisters."

She was right, they were uncomfortable. But up until that very moment those shoes had been my pride and joy, my ticket into the world of preteen. I'd waited two summers for those shoes and had spent over an hour polishing them with polish bought from my own allowance. There was no way I was going to give in on this one. "These are my favorite shoes! They're very comfortable! They're perfect for walking along the lake."

"You don't have to shout, dear, I was only thinking of you."

We walked down the hill in silence and headed on the shore path toward town. Two properties over was a brand new house that Grandma hadn't seen yet. "Wasn't this woods last time I was here?"

"Yes. They just finished this house last summer."

"This is where that charming little path used to wind through the woods. Remember, this is where those foxes used to live. The ones Barbara discovered."

"I found them first." I corrected her.

"No, it was Barbara. She always had such keen instincts about wildlife."

"No. I found the foxes first. You weren't even up here when we first saw them, so how would you know?" I was beginning to shout again.

"Oh never mind, it doesn't matter. I suppose they're all dead now that a house has been dropped on top of theirs."

It did matter. The foxes had been my discovery. It had been my keen eyes that first saw them, and my patience that had allowed me to see them again. I showed Barbara where they lived. Why couldn't Grandma remember that simple truth? I was angry at her and angry at the owners of the house for flushing out the foxes. We never saw them again. I hadn't thought about them in a long time and was suddenly overcome with sadness.

We walked on down to Mallory Spring. "Oh, I'm so glad this is still here, Grampy and I used to bring back gallons of water from here. Let's get a drink, it will make you feel better."

Yeah right, I thought. As if a swallow of water would bring back the foxes, or change the fact that Grandma totally refused to give me credit for my discovery. It was almost with pleasure that I announced, "Look at the sign, 'Unsafe to Drink.'"

"What happened? Spring water can't go bad. That's the stupidest thing I ever heard. Why don't they do something? They probably just don't want us on their property. What a shame."

We walked on in silence, each of us lost in our personal anger and sorrow. The joy of distant shouts and laughter from the boat traffic only seemed to deepen our anguish. A few water skiers glided by on the lake that was now calm as glass. I wanted to tell Grandma that I could water ski now, but I wouldn't waste more words. She really didn't care. The sun was dropping quickly and the mosquitoes started to swarm. "I think we need to go back, dear."

"Definitely."

The first star popped out. Grandma saw it before I did, and began the little poem "Star light, star bright, the first star I see tonight, I wish I may, I wish I might, have this wish I wish tonight." I said it along with her, under my breath, debating what I should wish for; the foxes to return to the lake or for Grandma to return to Chicago, or perhaps the return of Grandpa. That seemed far too big, no star could do that. Perhaps I'd wish that my mom would be home by the time we got back or that my dad would come back from Chicago a few days early. "Make a wish, hurry, before the other stars come out," Grandma insisted, startling me out of my reverie. Angrily I wished she would go away.

The house was dark as we climbed the hill up from the lake. Surely Mom should've been home by now. I was worried, but I didn't dare let on to Grandma. We were both hungry so we split the last can of tomato soup along with some stale crackers. After that we escaped into the world of sitcoms.

Mom popped in around nine o'clock. I knew she had spent too much time at the 19th hole, but hoped Grandma wouldn't notice. "Hi. Did you have a nice day together?"

"Oh, yes, Mom, Grandma bought me a new doll and a badminton set."

"Another one?" she giggled. I threw her a worried look. "Well, that's wonderful. You found something to eat, right?"

I looked at Grandma, my eyes pleading with her not to start a fight.

"Yes," she answered. "I'm very tired, I think I'll turn in now."

I woke up with a sense of sadness and dread the next morning; sadness about the foxes, and dread of spending another whole day alone with Grandma. As I opened my bedroom door I heard arguing downstairs.

"No one in this family is starving to death! Does Sandy look like she's starving for god's sake?"

"Quite frankly, she's scrawny as a rail. I'm truly worried." Scrawny? Boy did that hurt! I contemplated running off into the woods for the day. Maybe I'd find the foxes somewhere. Maybe they'd just moved to higher ground and hadn't died after all. That would make Grandma happy and then she'd know that my eyes were as good as Barbara's.

"She's just going through a growth spurt. She'll fill out."

I sat at the top of the stairs for a while, waiting for the storm to abate, then I crept trepidatiously down the stairs. They both seemed relieved at the distraction I offered. My mother placed a bowl, cereal and milk on the table for me, not her usual practice. I sat down and ate obediently.

"Is that all you want?" Grandma asked. "Can I make you some toast?"

"No thanks."

I ate slowly as Grandma looked on. Mom fluttered around the house busying herself. Then she came over and joined us. "I've got it," she stated with great satisfaction. Smiling at Grandma she said, "I'm going to let you do the cooking this week. You love to cook, you're marvelous at it, and you don't get much of a chance to cook anymore. You'd so enjoy that and Sandy would be more than willing to help you." Tom Sawyer at her best! I half expected her to get Grandma to pay her for the privilege. "I don't have time to take you shopping, but it doesn't matter. You can just call Power's grocery store and they'll deliver. Order whatever you want, and just charge it. Your son will be more than happy to pay the bill." Grandma just bit her lip while Mom placed the number by the phone and flew out the door. "Bye sweetie," she yelled as the screen door slammed.

Part of me wanted to fly out after her and beg to go along and part of me never wanted to see her again. "I'll do the dishes Grammy."

"Remember to rinse them carefully."

Grandma obtained pencil and paper and began to take an inventory of the cooking supplies in the kitchen. This took less time than it did to rinse my cereal bowl. Then she said, "You know your mother's idea is just brilliant." I figured she was trying to make me feel better, trying to hide her own anger at my mother. "It's certainly time for you to learn how to cook, and what better opportunity for me to pass the old family recipes down to you. We'll make goulash, chicken paprika, and cabbage rolls." She began vigorously writing a list of all the supplies we'd need. She was exuberant. It was like someone had shot her with a strong dose of amphetamines, although I didn't know what those were back then. After carefully compiling her list she called and ordered the food. They didn't have all the ingredients she'd hoped for, but she promised we'd make do.

"Nothing to do now but wait," she said, easing herself into one of the porch chairs.

"I'm going swimming," I announced.

"No dear, we need to wait for the groceries."

"Well, you can wait while I swim."

"Don't be ridiculous. Who'd pull you out if you'd start to drown?" Who'd pull me out anyway? The woman didn't know how to swim. I didn't dare remind her of that, though, it might have ended my swimming for the rest of the week.

"The groceries probably won't even get here until this afternoon. The guy just puts them in the kitchen. Mom never worries about it."

"There are a lot of things your mom never worries about. I have another surprise for you. Bring me that green shopping bag." Another surprise. This time I was downright fearful. Out of her bag she pulled her knitting needles strung with a large, half-finished pink baby sweater.

"Who's that for?"

"Why, you, of course. I remembered that pink is your favorite color." I hadn't ever remembered liking pink, in fact, I hated it. Grandma continued, "This wool is so fine, and I got it on sale." No surprise there. "I already finished Barbara's and I'd hoped to get yours done before I arrived. I'm really sorry. Anyway, if I work really hard, I might finish it while I'm here. You'll have it in time for school."

School? I was supposed to wear that thing in fifth grade? I'd look like a bundle fresh out of the nursery at Cook County Hospital. Surely Mom wouldn't make me wear it, but then free was free. Mom could be pragmatic at times.

"It's OK, Grammy, take your time."

Then, as if the situation wasn't bad enough, she said, "The best part, though, look, I've brought you your own knitting needles, and enough yarn so you can make a scarf."

"But, I don't know how. I'm not good at that sort of thing."

"Of course not! You've never had the opportunity to learn. Who better to teach you than me?"

"Girls don't do that kind of thing anymore, Grammy."

"Nonsense! Sit down and let's get started."

"I've got to brush my teeth first."

"That's fine. I'll get it started. Hurry back."

I carefully brushed each tooth, front, back and in between. I stared longingly down at the lake. If

Barbara had been here we'd have managed to defy Grandma, and slip right down to the lake anyway. If Grandpa had been here we'd have been swimming already. I felt a lump in my throat and fought off tears. I was beginning to understand what the big deal was about Grandpa.

Finally I returned to the porch. "Teeth all clean?" Grandma asked. Trust me, I thought.

She showed me how to hold the needles. It hurt. "Put the point through here, now loop, now pull. Easy. No, here. Careful. There you go. Oops. Try again. Not so hard. Just a little. Watch again. See, like this. Try it again. Not so much." Minute by minute I was confirming to Grandma what a hopeless case I was. "Dear, are you really trying?"

"Of course I am," I protested, holding back tears of frustration. Patiently Grandma repeated the whole process, showing me again and again. Finally I managed to finish a row.

"Now you're getting it. See? Keep going. I'll work on your sweater and you can continue on the scarf." Grandma seemed happy.

I continued until I had several rows done and I could start to visualize an actual scarf growing out of the process. I was feeling a little better about the whole thing.

"Hold it up," said Grandma. "Let me see it." I proudly held it up, knowing that she would smile approvingly at last. "You're getting the hang of it, but try to be more consistent, see how it's tighter here than over here. And you dropped a stitch, see, here. I'm just going to tear out a little bit, just to where you dropped the stitch."

"Pull it out? You mean I've got to do all that over again? Here!" I cried in disgust as I practically threw it at her. I ran up to my bedroom, slammed the door and beat my pillow. I planned on running away. I'd climb out the window and run into the woods. I'd take my blanket with me and just hide out until Grandma left. Maybe I'd find Barbara's Girl Scout camp and they'd sneak me into their cabin for a while. I had an address. It was somewhere in Illinois.

There was a knock at the front door. It was the man with the groceries. Grandma called up the stairs alerting me of the situation. I showed the guy where the kitchen was, and began to help Grandma put away the groceries. He came back in with a second box, and then a third, and still another. "We never get this much!" I said.

"You must be expecting a house full of company," the man said.

"No, just me and Grandma. But she means to fatten me up." He laughed, and smiled at me. I walked him out to the driveway. I wanted to beg him to take me on his rounds. I smiled and waved as he drove away.

"You need to be careful talking to strangers," Grandma said firmly.

I ignored her comment and asked, "Can I go swimming now?"

"Now it's time to start cooking lunch." She dove into the vegetables with gusto, the same way I longed to dive into the lake. She set up a chopping board, handed me a paring knife, and told me to get busy peeling and chopping. I'd never peeled an onion before. I was clumsy at it. My eyes were tearing.

"I can't do this, Grandma, it hurts too much."

"Run it under cold water, like this. Rinse your hands. Now, chop it like this. Down. Away from your hands."

After the onion there were peppers and carrots, celery and potatoes. I was clumsy at all of them, and far less patient than Grandma. "You really don't know how to cook, do you?"

"I can do some things; hot dogs, grilled cheese sandwiches, TV dinners. I'm good at eggs too."

"Well that's not cooking. By the end of the week you'll know how to do a whole lot more." I found no consolation in her optimism. Reluctantly I resigned myself that swimming wouldn't be on that day's agenda. It would take the rest of the morning just to finish cooking the vegetable soup. Then we'd have to eat it and digest it and do the dishes. By the time we'd done all this I suspected it would be time to start cooking dinner. Of course, I had to admit, even back then, that Grandma's vegetable soup was a whole lot tastier than peanut butter and jelly

Sure enough, by mid-afternoon we were at it again. Grandma had decided on chicken paprika. Although I hadn't eaten it in a few years, I had remembered loving it, and was amenable to the idea of learning to make it. First I had to watch as Grandma cut up a chicken and pulled out the little package of chicken guts. She held up each disgusting part, and my horror grew. "Here's the neck. Here's the liver. Here's the heart. Put them in a pan, we'll boil them and you'll see how tasty they are."

"Touch them? Oh gross. No. Please don't make me." I started to gag, for real. "Mom doesn't cook such gross stuff."

"Your mom doesn't cook, period." She put the slimy body parts in the pan herself. "Why don't you peel the skin off the breast and thighs?" I just stared at her in agony. "Oh, never mind. You know Barbara was never squeamish about cooking. She was actually getting quite good at it. I do need a couple of onions chopped. That's the least you can do."

I went and got my swim mask to protect my eyes. Grandma looked totally annoyed, but she kept her mouth shut. I couldn't see too well, but at least my eyes weren't burning. I was making good progress, making nice small bits. I was almost done when my finger got in the way. I sliced it, clean and deep. It bled like crazy, all over the onions. Grandma grabbed a tissue and held it tight around my finger. "It's that

stupid mask! You can't possibly see what you're doing! Where are the band aids?"

Grandma finished dinner without me, and I slipped out and took a very long walk, all the way to town and back. I got back to the house just as Mom was pulling into the driveway. I was so relieved to see her. We walked into the house together. "It smells great," she said. It did. "How come you're not helping Grandma?"

"I'm just not good at it," I started to explain about the onions as I followed her into the kitchen.

"What the devil!" she yelled. "Are you going to feed the Russian army? Who the hell is supposed to eat all of this food?"

Grandma was visibly crushed, and didn't even bother to reply.

"Well, I'm starving," I offered. "I'll set the table."

The dinner was superb. Grandma's cooking at its finest, as delicious as I'd remembered it. We tried complimenting her over and over, even Mom did, but the damage had been done. Mostly we ate in silence.

After dinner Mom turned on the TV. Grandma went to bed early. I went to my room and paged through Barbara's movie magazines.

When I climbed downstairs the following morning Mom's first words were, "Do you want to come along?"

"Where?"

"We're taking Grandma to the train station."

"But, it's not time, what about . . ."

"If you want to come it's got to be now, the train won't wait."

I had a million questions; like, why, and what about Dad coming on Friday, and what about all that food. I knew better than to ask. We drove to town in complete silence. I wanted to believe this was all Mom's fault, but I knew I hadn't been totally innocent either. I should've touched the bloody chicken parts, even if they grossed my out. I shouldn't have thrown my knitting at her. I should've thanked her for the old books. And then I remembered my wish on the star, and my guilt was complete. We helped carry Grandma's bags to the platform. The train was already loading.

"Thank you for having me," she said stonily to my mother. "Good-by dear," she said to me and climbed aboard.

One of my mother's country club buddies came up just then. She had dropped someone off too. "Say, I've got the decorations for Tuesday's luncheon in my car. Do you want to see them?"

"Of course, come on Sandy."

"But I want to watch the train pull away. Please Mom."

"Suit yourself. Just wait here. I'll be right back."

The powerful locomotive began chugging away slowly. I tried to see Grandma's face. I waved like mad at the dark windows. I stared as the train disappeared from sight. Its mournful whistle sounded in the distance and the old longing overtook me. I was left standing all alone on the platform, staring at the empty tracks as they reached off into infinity. It was eerily quiet. I stood there with tears pouring down my face. "You forgot to hug me, Grammy."

6

Birdsnest

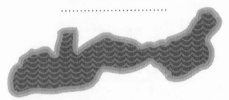

I don't think it was Friday the 13th, yet that might've explained that horrid Friday I experienced in mid-October. The date was close to that, in any event, as fall was in full swing. It had been the worst day yet of my miserable fifth grade school year. I started it by being late for school. A long and loud yelling from old Mrs. Applebaum, snickers from my classmates, and a trip to the principal's office followed. My dress had a small tear in it, no big deal, but the kids in my class found it very amusing, and made fun of it all day long. At recess I'd been kept indoors because I hadn't finished my math. Worst of all, though, was that I'd gotten caught red handed picking my nose, earning for myself the alliterative nickname, "Snot nosed Sandy." The kids in my class had a ball with that one. Debra DeVito passed out invitations to her birthday party; I didn't get one. Friday afternoon art class, usually the highlight of the week, proved disastrous after I spilled bright red paint all over Debra's beautiful picture. This got me more oral reprimands from both old Applebaum and Debra, dirty looks and sarcastic comments from Debra's entourage, and loss of my painting privilege. No one believed it was an accident. I spent the remainder of the afternoon sitting in the corner like a big dunce. My saving grace was that right after school we were going up to Lake Geneva. As soon as the bell rang, I ran all the way home.

I burst into the house shouting, "I'm home, let's go!"

"Slow down," my mother cautioned, "we're not going just yet."

"Why not?"

"Dad has to work late, that's all. We'll go after dinner."

Barbara, who'd arrived home five minutes before me, shouted with joy. "Great! I'm going to Nancy's house."

"Just be home in time for dinner, we'll leave right after that."

"After dinner! But I want to go now." I cried. "After dinner it will be dark. We won't get to see anything along the way and there'll be no time to play outside."

"Oh stop bellyaching! You're lucky to be going at all!" I stormed into my room and cried, the weight of the day crashing down on me.

By six o'clock my father had called to say he'd be another couple of hours. We ate without him. I thought I could speed things up by helping with the dishes, but broke one in my haste, earning yet another scolding. My mom shooed me away. I sulked in front of the TV, wishing I could drive away with Marty and Buzz of Route 66. I knew they'd be nice to me! It was after ten before we left. When we finally got to the lake, close to midnight, the air felt cold and thin. It smelled of wet leaves. The moon shone on the lake. I wanted to run down and feel the water, but my parents made me go to bed. Still, I was delighted to be up at the cottage. It was cold, but I snuggled down into my covers and felt warm, safe and cozy at last.

By the time I woke up, the sun was high in the sky. Brilliant gold shone through the windows. I couldn't wait to get out into the leaves. I got downstairs just in time to say good-by to my parents, who were off to the country club for the big closing weekend. "What time will you be back?" I asked.

"Late. You just go to bed before 10."

"You mean you won't be home for dinner?"

"No, we won't be home for dinner," she said in a whiney voice that reflected my own. "Don't whine! I bought your favorite TV dinner, fried chicken. There's also some ice cream left in the freezer." With that they were out the door.

I complained to Barbara. "They're going to be gone all day!"

"Yippee!" she said, as she cranked up WJJD on her transistor radio.

"So what are we going to do today?" I asked her, expecting her to come up with some exciting adventure.

"You act as though there actually is something to do up here this time of year! What did you have in mind?"

"We could go exploring, or something. It's so cool this time of year! With the leaves coming down you can see things we never get to see in summer."

"There's nothing left to explore; besides, I've got tons of homework. I've gotta do it before Monday."

"You're gonna do homework all day?" I asked in disgust.

"Just wait till you get to junior high, you'll see just how much homework you get." I didn't dare think about it, I was having enough trouble with fifth grade.

"I bet if your friend Donna comes over you won't be doing homework."

"No way Donna or anyone else is coming. No one comes up here this late in the season!"

"Well, this might be one of our last weekends too," I said, still hoping to convince her to come exploring with me.

"Hallelujah! Maybe next week I'll get to go to the movies with my friends!" She was hopeless. It was obvious that I would have to venture out alone. After a quick bowl of Cheerios I put on my old exploring jeans and shirt and took off. I went down to the lake first and climbed on the pier that sat in pieces on the shore. When we were small we used to pretend we were mountain climbing. I walked a little ways along the lakeshore noticing that all of the piers had already been taken in. It was so very very quiet. There was not a single boat on the lake. I walked toward town trying to see things up in the woods that weren't normally visible. I collected a bunch of pretty leaves to show Barbara. Last year we'd pressed some and taken them back to Chicago. I hoped Barbara would help me decide which ones were the best and then I'd show them to Mrs. Applebaum and earn some brownie points.

When I got back to the house I tried again to urge Barbara to come out and spend time with me. "I want to go on those big swings at the school house, why don't you come with me? You used to love them."

"Used to."

"The leaves are so neat this week, especially up on Snake Road, I'll bet. Why don't you come with me? Just take a little break."

"I've seen leaves before. I got homework, remember? Just let me do it." So I walked up to Woods School all by myself. The trees were brilliant all along the way. I swung so high my foot could almost reach the tree branches. I came even closer than Barbara had and I couldn't wait to tell her. After I grew bored swinging, I peeked into the windows of the little two-room schoolhouse, longing to be a student there. I was sure no one there would call me "Snot nosed

Sandy." I ambled slowly back toward home, wanting to be with Barbara, yet knowing I needed to leave her alone. When I got to the bend in the road I didn't take it toward home, but kept on going straight toward the Alta Vista farm. Black and white cows dotted the pasture. They were framed by the fall colors and the sparkling blue lake lie beyond all that. It looked like some of those post cards they sold at the Riviera. I watched the cows for a while and then walked on to the fork in the road. The road to the right was very familiar to me since my mom's golfing buddy, Helen Matthews lived down there, and Barbara hung out with her daughter Donna. We'd been there last summer for Donna's birthday. In addition to me and Barbara, they'd invited the neighbor kids and several other young teenagers from Big Foot Country Club. I was the youngest one there and bored out of my mind. The whole thing turned into an embarrassing boy girl party where they played dumb games, giggled, flirted and acted stupid. The mothers acted equally stupid as they sat back, watching, drinking, giggling and gossiping about their precious young adolescents. Needless to say, I had no desire to head down that road. I took the fork to the left. I was curious what I might find. It led into thick woods where the leaves streamed down like confetti with every gust of wind. After a while I came to a crooked little white cottage. There was a rusty pickup truck in the driveway, junk everywhere, and a magnificent tire swing hanging from a tall tree.

I walked past the swing slowly, wishing I had one. Suddenly I got the weirdest feeling, like something was looking at me. I quickened my pace.

"Hey, do you want to go on my tire swing?" I turned around startled and saw a curly headed girl, about my age, coming toward me.

"Sure, I'd love to go on your tire swing." I replied.

"I'm Bobby Jo," she said, as I climbed into the tire.

"I'm Sandy." She swung me so high, and the tire spun around, until I was deliciously dizzy. After the world stopped spinning, I did the same for her. We kept taking turns until our stomachs could take no more.

"You wanna jump in the leaves?" she asked me.

"Sure," I answered. She picked up a rake and gathered a huge pile of leaves. We ran and jumped over and over, eventually adding spins, cartwheels and even flips. After a while we moved on to building leaf houses and she showed me how to make miniature pots and pans out of acorns.

"Hey, do you wanna see our kittens?" she asked. Of course I did. I'd never seen newborn kittens before. We entered the back door of the cottage. The little entryway was crammed with mops and brooms. We had to squeeze past them. We entered a small kitchen that reeked of wine and garlic. Her mother was standing at the stove stirring a huge pot. "My mom's making grape jelly," Bobby Jo was quick to explain.

"Well, hi there," her mother said to me. She gave me a big smile, which looked a little scary due to her bony face and crooked front teeth. She had hair as curly as Bobby Jo's, but it was stringier and jet-black. Her arms were so skinny you could hardly tell where the wooden spoon ended and her arm began. I wasn't sure if she was very tall or if the cottage was very short. Either way, her head almost hit the ceiling. "Maybe you can take a pint of grape jelly home with you after they cool," she suggested.

"Thank you," I said, politely. There were other jars sitting on the table cooling. I was curious about them, but too afraid to ask. She must've read my mind.

"Those jars are my homemade cough medicine. I put in whiskey, lemon juice, peppermint and garlic.

You should tell your mom about it. It works better than any of the store bought remedies and is much less expensive and much better for you."

"I will," I lied. "Where are the kittens?"

We went into a small shabbily furnished living room and there in the corner was a box of adorable black kittens. They'd just opened their eyes. I got to pick them up and let them lick milk off my finger. I so wanted to take one home. After playing with the kittens for a while we watched as her mother strained the jelly and ladled it into the jars. Then she fixed us cucumber sandwiches on homemade bread and apple slices with sugar and cinnamon.

After lunch Bobby Jo asked me if I liked to climb trees. No girl had ever asked me that before. She led me on further down the road toward the lake. Then we cut through some thick woods and eventually reached a hill overlooking the lake. There was a magnificent tree with branches close together, perfect for climbing. "Follow me," she said. She scooted up the tree like a monkey. I followed, much more slowly. Before long we were sitting way up near the top of the tree. It felt even higher than it was because it was on the edge of a hill. The sun was glistening off the lake making it look like it was covered in diamonds. We sat up there for a long time feeling the wind in our faces.

"How come I've never seen you before?" I asked.

"I don't know."

"Have you lived here long?"

"We moved here last April, after my dad came home."

"Was he in the army or something?"

"He was working for the government. Some top secret spy stuff with the Soviet Union. But don't ever tell anyone, I'd be in trouble if he knew I told you. He's not allowed to talk to anyone about it, not even me and my mom."

"Wow. Was he away a long time?'

"Yeah, Mom and me lived with my grandma."

"Did he get to come home at Christmas?"

"Nope. It would've been too dangerous for him to come home. We weren't allowed to see him at all."

"Well, I bet you're glad that's over."

"Yeah, but I miss my grandma."

"Do you get to live here year round?" I asked her.

"Yeah, this is where we live now. My dad works for the big farm and we get to live in the house for free." There were so many more questions I wanted to ask about her dad, but I didn't want to get her in trouble.

"You're so lucky. I wish I lived here year around. Hey, that must mean you go to Woods School. I've always wanted to go there. What's it like?"

"I hate school. I miss my best friend from my old school. I'm the only girl in fifth grade." She looked sad and contemplative for a few seconds, and it was clear I'd dug a little too deep. She began scrambling down the tree. "Come on, let's go!" she said.

We walked along the shore path for a short while, and then followed an old creek bed away from the lake. We discovered an old abandoned bridge, and then found ourselves back up near Woods School. She was not eager to play there, but I convinced her we'd have fun, and we did. We must have weighed about the same because we were perfectly balanced on the seasaws and the high fliers. We soared like birds and I heard her laugh for the first time. On the swings we raced to see who could touch the tree branches first, though neither of us could do it. After we slowed down she said, "I wish you went to school here with me."

"So do I! I hate my school, the kids are so mean."

"Some of the kids here are mean too. They call me names." She looked sad again and I wanted to cheer her up.

"They call me 'Snot nosed Sandy,'" I told her, hoping it would help.

She looked at me with sympathetic eyes and suddenly perked up, "Hey, can you keep a secret?"

"Sure," I promised.

"I'm gonna take you to my private club house, but you've got to promise never to tell anyone about it." I promised, and we began running down Snake Road. I struggled to keep up with her and suddenly I tripped and found myself sprawled on the pavement. I'd ripped a hole in my jeans and had blood trickling down from my knee.

"Bobby Jo, wait up," I yelled. This brought her running back. When she saw my knee a big smile crossed her face.

"Hey, we can become blood sisters!" Quickly she unpinned the safety pin that held her shirt closed and jabbed herself on the thumb. She pushed out the blood and then, before I had time to consent or object, she put it on my knee, mixing our blood together. "Now we're blood sisters! We're one forever and ever 'cause we share each other's blood!" Then she pinned her shirt closed, helped me off the pavement and linked her arm with mine. She continued to smile, and we began skipping down the road with our arms linked, singing *Follow the Yellow Brick Road*. We passed the cows again with the shimmering lake behind. Bobby Jo told me they were Holsteins and she began identifying them by name. There was Beulah, Daisy, Cupcake, Bubba and a host of others. I wasn't sure if she really could tell them apart or if she was just making all of this up. "Have you ever watched cows being milked?" she asked me.

"No, I've never seen it."

"They'll be milking them around 6 o'clock tonight. My dad works there and he lets me watch as long as I stay out of the way, and the owner's not around. Maybe we can watch them tonight," she suggested. We continued walking toward her house, but took a turn on a dirt road just before we got there. We walked along the edge of a field until we came to a strange little building, maybe it was an old chicken-coupe or something. Before Bobby Jo opened the door she made me pinky promise as her blood sister that I would never ever tell anyone about this secret spot, cross my heard and hope to die, stick a needle in my eye, and everything else she could think of. I'm not sure what I was expecting to find, but I was totally surprised when she opened the door. There were big windows that were really dirty, but the afternoon sun beat down on them making the little building light and warm. There were three shelves, probably where chickens once roosted, or maybe they had started trays of seedlings there in the spring. The middle shelf held a bunch of old paint tubes, some jars full of paint, and a bunch of brushes. The other shelves were covered with paintings. They were mostly fall scenes, but there were also paintings of the lake and paintings of barns and some really good horses.

"Wow! Who painted these?" I asked.

"Me," she said, beaming with pride.

"These are really good! Nobody in my class can paint this good, not even Debra DeVito!"

"You wanna paint a picture?" she asked. I was kind of anxious to paint, especially since I didn't get to the day before at school and it felt like I'd sort of be getting back at my teacher. But I was embarrassed to paint in front of Bobby Jo; her stuff was so good.

"But I'm so bad at it," I answered.

"It's OK, I'll show you a few secrets." She carefully set up paper and squeezed some paint out of each tube onto a little board. She taught me how to paint some simple roses, and showed me how to blend colors. I filled several papers with colorful roses. We painted for a long time, until the sun dropped below the tree line and we could no longer see very well. Then she carefully cleaned the brushes using water from an old milk bottle. Over and over she rinsed the brushes and then wiped them clean on her shirt.

"It's getting dark, I think I'd better get home," I said, reluctantly.

"Do you have to? Don't you want to go see the cows being milked?" I hesitated. The later I got home, the happier Barbara would be, and my folks, not due in till after ten, would never know the difference. I didn't want to leave, but I was scared of walking home after dark. I remembered just how pitch black dark it was at night.

"I'd better go. I'm supposed to be home before dark."

"But you'll be back tomorrow, right?"

"Sure," I promised.

"If you come at 6 o'clock in the morning we can watch the milking. I know where there's a dead sheep in the woods, I'll show it to you. And if the owner's not around, we can play in the hayloft at the farm. I'm gonna paint a picture for you too. You'll be here, right?"

"Of course," I promised, again.

'Blood sisters always tell the truth to each other. Pinky promise! We will meet again tomorrow!" she announced as we hooked our pinkies together. She gave me another big, happy smile.

I thought I'd cut off some distance by cutting across the field. As I crossed, I turned and waved several times. Each time I turned around it seemed that Bobby Jo grew smaller and more raggedy, her curly hair in a gnarled heap on top of her head. She stood there the whole time and we gave each other one last big wave before I entered the woods. I hoped to discover some cool things that I could share with her the next day, but it was getting dark fast. My short cut was not helpful at all as it was slow going in the woods and I lost my direction. I did finally come back out onto Snake Road, but I still had half a mile to go. I wished Bobby Jo were with me. She probably wasn't afraid of the dark. I ran the rest of the way racing against the setting sun. I was relieved to see light coming from our cottage, which guided me down the last hill and right to our door. I couldn't wait to tell Barbara about my day. For once I'd had a more exciting day than her!

"Where've you been?" she screamed at me. "It's dark!"

"Why are you so angry? " I asked, a little bewildered.

"Mom and Dad would kill me if they knew how late you were out! Where've you been?"

"I met a new friend. We were playing all day, and I got to see baby kittens . . ."

"But where, where did you go?"

"I was with Bobby Jo, she lives over by the Alta Vista Farm."

"Not Birdsnest!" she said, horrified.

"What are you talking about?"

"That cootie girl that lives over there! You were playing with Birdsnest?"

"She's not a cootie girl," I objected.

"Don't you remember the kids talking about her last summer at Donna's party? She's dirty and disgusting and smelly. She's always covered in paint." I looked down at my paint covered pants and shirt, and Barbara continued, "She's got curly hair that sits on top of her head like a bird's nest. She's a fifth grader at Wood's School. She lives in that white cottage."

"She's not dirty and disgusting! She's my friend!"

"You idiot!!! She's horrible. Don't ever play with her. You know what kind of reputation you'll get if you do? Everyone will start looking at *you* as a cootie girl!" I wasn't quite sure who "everyone" was, and I wasn't quite sure if it mattered much.

"I don't care," I said, proudly.

"Did you know that her mother is a witch?"

"That's ridiculous," I answered. Then I thought about her mother's stringy black hair and bony face. I thought about her home made cough potion and remembered how she looked stirring that huge cauldron. I thought about all the brooms at the back door and the black kittens. But surely, there were no such things as witches. "Her mother was really nice to me! She even fixed lunch for me!"

"Oh my god, you didn't eat over there, did you? You'll be lucky if you don't get sick, or turn into a frog or something."

"Oh, stop it!" Now I knew she was going over-board. "Even if she is a witch, it doesn't matter. Bobby Jo's my friend, not her mother."

"Her dad is an ex con! Don't you remember last summer when Mrs. Matthews and all those other women were talking about him? They're all upset that he was hired and they're trying to get him out of there. Why those kids that live over there have been ordered never never never even to go past their house or even near the farm now that he's working there. Man, Mom and Dad are gonna kill you when they find out you were over there!"

Then I laughed. "No, no, her dad's not an ex con, he worked . . ." I stopped short, because I remembered that I'd promised Bobby Jo I wouldn't say anything about her dad's secret work. Then I got to thinking how weird it was that some top government guy would go to be a hired hand on a farm. It didn't make a lot of sense. Still, I didn't want to believe Barbara. Maybe she was thinking of some other guy.

"Are you sure? What did he do?" I asked.

"I don't know, they wouldn't tell us, but he spent five years in prison for it! Ryan, that kid that lives next door to Donna, he says it was for helping his wife collect children's eye balls."

"Ryan's a moron!" I protested. Still, Barbara's words were beginning to scare me. I hadn't put it all together before, but now that she'd mentioned it, I had a vague recollection of the mothers at the birthday party talking about some ex con. When we'd all been instructed not to go "over there" it hadn't really registered with me where "over there" was. It hadn't been any concern of mine because I didn't live there.

Barbara ended with, "Just don't go over there. He might rape you or kill you or something!"

I didn't take Barbara too seriously that evening, in fact I'd hoped to wake up early and walk over to watch the cows being milked. Of course it was still dark at that hour, so that surely didn't happen. Barbara hadn't said anything to my parents who returned to the country club on Sunday morning. I kind of hung around for a while, ate breakfast, sorted my leaf collection, and then reluctantly headed back up toward Bobby Jo's house.

The weather had turned cold and overcast. I started out walking toward Snake Road, but decided to run back and get some warmer clothes. I spent a long time deciding whether to wear my sweatshirt or my jacket. I started walking again, thinking about what to say to Bobby Jo. I'd find out the real truth from her and her parents and straighten out the whole mess. But I would be embarrassed to ask her, and she probably wouldn't want to talk about it anyway. In fact, the thought struck me, maybe she didn't even know the truth. Maybe her parents and grandmother lied to her all those years. But it was also possible that he had been some kind of secret agent, and maybe the ex con story was used just to cover up his secret spy work. I got all the way up to Snake Road, but then decided I shouldn't go past the farm where her dad worked. If Barbara's story was true he might actually be dangerous. What if he saw me and decided to rape me or something? I would go along the lake path instead, and go to her house that way. I kept thinking about Bobby Jo, knowing she was waiting for me. I promised I'd come, but I hadn't said what time.

I stopped back at our cottage to grab something to eat. I ate slowly. I started walking along the lake and thought about Bobby Jo's mom. She'd want to give me a jar of jelly. Should I tell her I can't accept jelly from a witch? If I took a jar, how could I explain that to my mom? Maybe I would just ditch it in the woods somewhere. But if she really was a witch she'd probably know I did it and cast some kind of spell on me. I got close to the spot where we'd climbed up the tree. I longed to climb it again, but I wasn't sure I could find it, and it wouldn't be as much fun alone.

It started to drizzle. If I went to Bobby Jo's house we'd have to play indoors. Her witchy mother would be there, and maybe her ex con secret agent dad as well. I went back home instead. Barbara was watching a movie. I watched it with her. By the time it was over the drizzle had ceased. There still would have been time for me to get to Bobby Jo's. I thought maybe I would just sneak back through the woods directly to her clubhouse. Maybe she'd be there and I wouldn't have to see either one of her parents. It was sort of a long shot.

Then I thought about her messy clothes and her bird's nest hair, and her terrible reputation. Did she actually smell bad? I hadn't remembered that. I wondered what Debra DeVito and all her friends would say if they knew I had a friend like Birdsnest. Barbara would be forever on my case and her friend Donna would call me a cootie girl. All the country club women would be aghast. My mom would outright forbid it. I hesitated. Something else came on TV. I sat and watched. Then I watched whatever else came on. Eventually my parents were home and we were packing up for the ride back to the city.

I thought about Birdsnest all the way home. I'd promised her I'd come but I'd broken my promise. I felt horrible. I decided I'd have to talk my dad into returning the next week. I'd visit Bobby Jo on Saturday and make it up to her. I wasn't sure exactly what I would tell her, but I'd come up with some story, and then let her know how sorry I was. I'd bring her a little gift too, maybe one of my stuffed animals, or maybe one of my books.

The next weekend, however, we did not return to the lake. In fact, we didn't return until May. The first

chance I got, I headed over to her house. This time
I'd be more discreet; there was no need to tell Barbara anything. Even if someone found out, I didn't
care. I'd lived with a bad conscience all winter long
and whatever might happen to me couldn't be worse
than that. The ground smelled damp. The leaves were
mostly out, but still in their light green stage. Apple
blossoms were in full bloom. I felt light and clean
and new. I couldn't wait to see Bobby Jo. Maybe we'd
finally get to play in the hayloft. I was giddy thinking that in just about six weeks we'd be up for the
whole summer. Then I could see Bobby Jo every
day. For once I'd have a friend my age to play with.
Even if my parents forbade it, I'd sneak over there
in secret. That thought made it even more exciting.

I began to run as I approached her cottage. The
first thing I noticed when I got there was that the
tire swing was gone. In fact, the yard looked empty.
I ran up to the house and noticed it was padlocked.
No one could possibly be inside. I peeked through the
window. The house was empty. I felt awful. I wanted
to ask someone where she'd gone and how I could
find her, but there was no one around to ask. I walked
slowly toward her clubhouse. I'd promised I'd never
tell anyone else about it, but I didn't see any harm
in visiting it myself. Old leaves blown up against the
door told me no one had entered it for quite a while. I
pushed the leaves away with my foot and pulled open
the door. I was surprised to see it pretty much as I'd

remembered it. Her paints and brushes were still there. The bottle that had held her water was cracked and empty, like it had frozen and broken over the winter. The paints probably were ruined as well. I couldn't believe she'd just left everything. She loved her paints so much, and she'd been so careful about cleaning her brushes. Maybe they had to leave suddenly and she didn't have time to come back for her stuff. I hoped she hadn't gotten sick or something. Her pictures were still lying around too. I looked at them again, in awe at how skilled she was. Then I found one I hadn't seen before. It was a beautiful fall scene with two girls standing inside of a heart. The words printed on it were, "To Sandy, my best friend ever, Love, Bobby Jo."

Letters from Laura

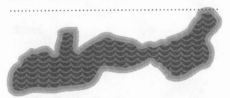

"It's a big one, a really big one!" yelled little Brucey exuberantly. I watched him reel it in like it was the most important matter on earth. He pulled up a little perch.

"Nice one!" I yelled, hoping he wouldn't be too disappointed. It's got to be at least seven inches. It's one of the biggest I've seen. Your grandpa's gonna be so proud. Nice addition to our feast tonight!" Brucey was the little neighbor kid. His grandparents had bought Mrs. Murphy's house. He always fished off of our pier claiming that the fish were better over there. I think it had more to do with the protective roof which shielded us from the rain. Either way, the arrangement was favorable to us both. Even though Brucey was five years younger than I, I appreciated his company. It was a cool, drizzly morning, the kind that promised biting fish.

Over the still water we could hear the clear voice of the tour guide on a sightseeing boat. Before it

came into view I said, "Guess which one that is, hurry before it comes around the corner."

"Easy. At this time of morning it's got to be the Walworth. Maybe you'll get mail." To our delight the boat came around the point and headed straight for our pier. As the boat glided past I stuck out my hand, receiving the mail like the perfect passing of a baton. The tourists cheered and Brucey and I waved as they pulled away.

To my delight I discovered a letter from my best friend Laura. I eagerly tore it open.

Dear Sandy,

I wish I could come to visit but I have to baby-sit every single morning while my mom's at work. You can't imagine how boring and bratty 8 year olds are. I can't wait for high school to start. At least I've got WLS to listen to. Can you get it up there? Have you heard Little Old Lady from Pasadena? It's the greatest.

As soon as my mom gets home, Carol and I are going up town to get the WLS Silver Dollar Survey. I'll pick you up one if they let me take an extra. I can't wait to see if Hard Day's Night is still number one. Me and Melissa and Carol and Karen are all going to see the movie on Saturday. Have you seen it yet?

I'm also going to look for a mohair sweater to match my new navy blue plaid skirt. My mom's been paying me well, so I've been able to get a lot of cool new clothes for high school. I wish you could see them.

I'm signing my name with my new cherry blossom lipstick. Don't you just love the color? I can't wait to wear it to school.

Love,
Laura

The letter churned me up. What was she doing hanging around Karen and Melissa? They were part of the "it" crowd, totally out of our league. And what was wrong with me that I couldn't have cared less about clothes or make-up. I wondered what I'd be able to write back. Would I tell her I'd spent the last three cold, rainy days sticking worms on hooks, in the company of an eight year old? Would I tell her we caught a whole slough of fish, that the old neighbor man cut off their heads and pulled out their guts and that tonight we'd get to eat them? Would I tell her the battery on the transistor radio she'd given me was dead, and I hadn't bothered to replace it? Would I tell her the only music I heard was the tweeting of robins, the call of the cat bird, and the din of motor boats? I concentrated on the sound of an approaching outboard.

Brucey yelled, "Hey! Look at that cool Boston whaler. He was obsessed with them that summer. I thought they were pretty cool too. The little boat pulled up right in front of the pier. The driver shifted into neutral and yelled out, "Hey, do you know a good fishing spot?"

Brucey pointed to the little cove just west of us, "You might catch some bass in there. There's lots of seaweed in there, they like that. Nice boat!"

"Thanks," he replied with a smile that could melt butter.

"Nice, huh?" Brucey said to me.

"Oh yeah! Nice. Really gorgeous." I didn't understand the sensation that was overtaking me. We continued staring as the boat moved into the cove and dropped anchor. But I wasn't lusting after the boat. It was the driver that had taken my breath away. It was driven by the most gorgeous creature I'd ever laid eyes on. He had blonde hair, blue eyes, a dream boat face and a golden tan, a surfer from Malibu, no doubt. Home coming king. Surely every girl in his school swooned over him, but of course, only the most popular ones would be able to get near him.

Then it hit me. I was the only girl around! This beautiful creature sat all alone, alone in his Boston whaler. Surely he needed a companion. Why hadn't I thought more quickly, been braver and offered to ride with him over to the cove? I was kicking myself until I realized just what a mess I was. I was dressed in my old jeans and my dad's old raincoat. My hair was a stringy, wet mess. I hoped he hadn't gotten too close a look at me.

I continued to gape long after he dropped anchor, but I could not see his face. I had to have another look. "I'm sick of fishing," I announced. "You can have the rest of the night crawlers." I deposited my fishing pole in the house, grabbed the binoculars, and snuck out the back and around the neighbor's house to the shore path, hoping no one would see me. I followed the shore path toward the cove. It climbed up into a patch of woods where I was confident that my dad's green raincoat would camouflage me. I perched myself in the lower branches of a tree that stood overlooking the lake. There he was, sitting like an angel, with his pole in the water. I held up my binoculars for a closer look, perfect. I wondered if he could feel me staring. I sent kisses through the air.

I named him Adonis. We'd studied about him in English class. Venus had been captivated by his beauty and cared for nothing else, just like me. I was hopelessly overcome with a need to kiss this guy. I didn't kiss guys, unless you count playing spin the bottle with your cousins as kissing. Those were mostly pecks of torture, not something I longed for. I'd just finished eighth grade, but had never had a boyfriend. I really didn't care; all the guys in my school were stupid, ugly, or stuck up. Adonis was different.

I stared for a long time. I was getting sore. I tried to shift my position. I wanted to melt into his arms. I closed my eyes, I was swooning toward him. Suddenly I lost my balance and tumbled to the ground. I lay there feeling stupid. I hoped I hadn't broken Mom's binoculars or torn Dad's raincoat. Worse, I feared that if Adonis had seen it or heard it he'd think I was a clumsy fool. My clothes were wet and coated with mud and leaves. My back hurt. I stood up and positioned myself for another look at Adonis. The binoculars had not been damaged, but now he was facing out toward the lake. I couldn't see his angelic face. "Come

on, sweetheart, turn your face. I must see you again!"
I waited for a long time, but he didn't cooperate. It
began to rain harder. He pulled in his line, started the
motor and cruised out of the cove. An urge to follow
him overtook me. I had to know where he was staying. I ran along the path, trying to catch up. I rounded
the point, but it was too late. The boat was nowhere to
be seen. Sadly, I wandered back to the house.

I sent Laura a postcard so I wouldn't have to write
too much.

> Dear Laura,
> I'm sorry you can't come up to
> visit.
> Your letter came this morning by
> boat, the one on the front of this
> postcard. I met a really cute guy.
> Tonight we're going to a fish fry.
>
> Love Sandy

I set my thoughts on Adonis. I wondered where
he was from, where he was staying, and what year
he was in school. Did he have a girlfriend? What
a stupid question, of course he did, probably ten of
them. Still, I just had to see him again. I looked in
the mirror and was embarrassed at the immature
mess that stared back. If I was going to win over a guy

of Adonis's caliber I'd have to make some changes. I hiked to town. I spent a good deal of my eighth grade graduation money on a sexy, bright yellow bikini. I also bought some make-up and batteries for my transistor radio. I began curling my hair every night. I started to do sit ups. I skipped breakfast and swore off of ice cream. Every day in my sexy bikini I'd march down to the pier, all made up, binoculars and transistor radio in hand, waiting and watching for Adonis. I was just sure he'd come by again. I got another letter from Laura,

Dear Sandy,

You won't believe this, but last Sunday Carol and Melissa and Karen and I were hanging out in the school yard. Anthony Puccilli came over with two other really cool guys and asked us to play baseball with them. Yes, Anthony! Cool, gorgeous Anthony! We had so much fun. Since then we've been playing baseball and hanging out every single evening after supper. Last night he walked me home. We sat out on the front porch talking for a long time, until my dad made me come in. He said he likes me, and I'm totally flipped over him. He probably would've kissed me if my dad hadn't come out so soon. Tell me more about the guy you met. What's his name? What does he look like? Details, please.

By the way, I hate fish.

Hard Day's Night was so great. And did you know that the Beach Boys are number one this week? I Get Around is just the greatest song.

Love, Laura

I was angry and envious. Anthony was the epitome of gorgeous and cool, but not for Laura. We'd always talked about how conceited he was.

Dear Laura,

I'm glad you're having such a great summer. That's so totally cool that you're hanging around Anthony. Maybe he'll take you to the homecoming dance. Has he kissed you yet?

We've been swimming, and skiing every day, and sunbathing to WLS. Isn't it just the coolest? I wish you could see the new yellow bikini I bought. It's really pretty, and kind of low cut. My dad hasn't seen it yet. I hope he doesn't.

Details, here goes. His name
is Don. He's 15. He is absolutely
gorgeous and so nice. He's a surfer
from Malibu. He's visiting his uncle,
who owns one of the mansions on
this lake. He has a really cool boat
and he takes me zooming around the
lake with him every day. He likes
my bikini. How is it going with
Anthony? Has he kissed you yet?

Love, Sandy

In the meantime, I was getting a little impatient
waiting for Adonis to come back. I decided I had to
be a little more aggressive. I would have to find him. I
walked from the narrows, all the way to Williams Bay,
a distance of at least three miles, looking for his boat.
I saw nine Boston Whalers, just like his, but no sign
of him. I decided I'd just walk that path every single
day until I found him. Laura wrote back to me.

Dear Sandy,
     Anthony and I went to the show. We
saw "From Russia with Love." Have you
seen it yet? I cried it was so beautiful,
and Anthony put his arm around me

and was so very very sweet. Yes, of
course, we have kissed, but don't tell my
mom. I think he's going to ask me to go
steady.

Love, Laura

I'd gone to see *Mary Poppins* with Brucey, but I
didn't tell her that, instead I wrote,

Dear Laura,
   I'm glad it's going so well with
Anthony. Don and I haven't been to a
movie yet. Mostly we just spend time
in his boat. Usually we anchor over at
Black Point and make out. He kisses so
good. Last night we went swimming in
the moonlight off of our pier.

Love, Sandy

I woke up to yet another rainy day. I didn't bother
with the make-up and the whole bit, and passed on
my habitual walk to try to find Adonis. I was losing
patience. Brucey was down on our pier fishing again,
but I opted to stick my nose in a book. I sat on the
porch enveloped in the stillness and quiet of the
morning. I heard a motor and looked down at the
lake. Oh my goodness, there was the whaler! Should

I run down or should I run upstairs first and make myself up? He was tying up. Quickly I ran upstairs and put on the coolest shirt I owned. I combed my hair and put on a dab of lipstick. I began racing down to the pier, but slowed myself not wanting to look like a foolish kid. My heart was pounding as I approached. Adonis and Brucey were involved in a conversation. Maybe he was asking about me, wondering if I were available, how old I was, stuff like I wondered about him. He was a little shorter than I had imagined, of course he'd been sitting.

"Hi," I said, offering him my sexiest smile, "I'm Sandy. What's your name?"

"Hi, I'm Edwin."

"Edwin?" I was a little shocked, but tried not to show it.

With a mouth much larger than the one I remembered, he replied, "Yes, Edwin Samuelson the third."

"So, Edwin Samuelson the third, where are you staying?"

"Over at Knollwood, my uncle's renting a cabin over there." I had the uncle part right at least. He turned to continue talking with Brucey.

"Where are you from?" I interrupted.

"Hyde Park."

"You mean, the Hyde Park in Chicago? You're from Chicago?"

"Yeah, is that so strange?"

"Oh, no, of course not. Everybody up here is from Chicago. Do you go to Hyde Park High?"

"No," he laughed. "I go to Bret Harte Elementary."

I couldn't have heard that right. "What grade are you in?"

"I'm going into fifth."

Brucey chimed in, "Edwin and I are going fishing, soon as I tell Grandma. We're gonna try to catch some Northern Pike, maybe over at Black Point."

"Oh, great," I said, trying to hide my shock and disappointment. "People catch all kinds of stuff over there, have fun." I turned and walked slowly up the hill.

Dear Laura,

I'm so glad you and Anthony are going steady. I can't write much because I'm so very very sad and heart broken. Don had to go back to Malibu. But he promised to write, and gave me a ring which I'll wear forever."

Love, Sandy

8

Awakening

....

"Yo ho HO and a bottle of rum!" Brucey and I chanted, over and over, as we rowed toward Skeleton Island. On the third "ho" we pulled the oars together. It helped us stay coordinated, no small feat considering the difference in our size and strength. When we approached the island he took his place in the bow of the rowboat. "Careful over the reef now men!" he ordered.

"Aye, aye, Captain Smollet!" I answered as I maneuvered the boat into the little bay in front of the Wychwood Estate. Brucey perched himself in the bow of the rowboat examining the shoreline carefully with his spyglass in search of pirates or cannibals. He looked so cute with the paper towel roll smashed against his eye and the pirate hat on his head, the one I'd made from a page of the Wall Street Journal.

When he was satisfied that no one was around he yelled, "The coast is clear, Doc." Then I rowed around to the side of the island not visible from the house and as close to the shore as I could get. Brucey leapt off the boat onto the shore, the perfect location for playing pirates.

"Good luck to ya, Captain Smollet," I yelled, and he ran across the private island quickly, hoping not to be seen by anyone. After he crossed the bridge and climbed over the chain with the "No Trespassing" sign on it he raced me back home. Of course he won. It was hard rowing all that way, with the wind and current against me. As soon as I got home, he made me walk the plank. The diving board served this purpose well and I welcomed a dunk in the lake.

On other occasions the diving board became the deck of the Hispaniola. Paper towel rolls turned into spyglasses, guns or swords. Brucey loved playing pirates even more than he loved fishing. Often I would hide treasure for Brucey and draw him a treasure map. If I were lazy I'd hide it close by, like in his grandparents' back yard. Other days I was more ambitious and I'd hide something up in the woods or fields and draw more elaborate maps. On those days I took on the role of Ben Gunn, I probably looked about as unkempt. Ben Gunn and Jim Hawkins would be off on a dangerous adventure, avoiding pirates and searching for buried treasure. The treasure usually consisted of a few coins, a few pieces of candy, or some old toy we had sitting around which I'd put in a tin box. The treasure itself didn't matter to Brucey; he just wanted to play.

I was delighted at my ability to make Brucey happy. No one had ever appreciated me quite as much as he did. I was also glad to be able to share my love of books with someone. His vivid imagination combined with my own made the classics come alive. I wished I could tell my freshman English teacher. She'd turned me on to the classics, which was really amazing considering I'd never enjoyed reading before. Years earlier my grandmother had dumped off a bunch of old classics, which sat unread on a shelf growing steadily mustier and moldier. Suddenly I discovered them, like some lost treasure, buried under my very nose. I'd planned on reading as many as I could over the summer.

All was well and good, except for one thing, my mother. "Are you sure you're going to be alright?" she asked me for about the fourth time one morning before she left for the country club. I was curled in my favorite chair with my nose stuck in *Treasure Island*. I wished she'd just leave so I could get back to my reading.

"Yes, Mom, I'll be fine!" I couldn't understand why she was acting so weird. She'd been golfing since I was six, and had never worried about leaving me before.

"Well, you're sure now?"

"YES! For the 100th time! YES!"

"Hey, don't yell at me! It's just that Barbara's working all day and I won't be back until late this afternoon. I don't want you to get lonely."

"Well, thanks, Mom, but, really, I want to finish this book and I've got others waiting. You'll be home before I finish them, I promise. Anyway, Brucey will no doubt stop by later."

When she got home I was curled up in the same chair. "Have you gotten out of that chair since I left?" she asked me in a rather disgusted tone.

"Yes, Mom. Brucey stopped by and we searched for treasure up in the meadow and we killed at least a dozen pirates. I'm tired now, for obvious reasons, and I just want to relax with my book."

A few days later she arrived home to find me curled up in my favorite chair reading *Moby Dick*. "Are you still in that chair? Have you left it at all today?"

"Yes, Mom. Me and Brucey went whale hunting earlier, but he had to go in for dinner, and I'm hoping to finish this book soon." She just looked at me with a sort of worried expression.

A few days later she came home and found me in the same chair reading *Swiss Family Robinson*. "Please don't tell me you've spent all day reading again." So I said not a word while she stared down at me. "Well, did you?"

"Did I what?"

"Did you spend another whole day in that chair reading?"

"No, Mom, Brucey and I got shipwrecked and ended up building a really nifty fort! I'll show it to you if you want to see it."

"Honey, I don't like what's happening to you. How come you're not out water skiing or something?"

"Well, Mom, to tell you the truth, I'd love to be out water skiing, but as of yet, I can't figure out how to drive the boat, handle the rope, and water ski all at the same time. But when I do, you'll see me buzzing around out there when you get home from the golf course."

"Look! Don't you get snippy with me, young lady! I'm trying to help you. It's just not healthy at your age for you to be alone all day reading books. You ought to be hanging out with your friends and doing things, like Barbara." This was preposterous. Ordinarily she ran non-stop complaints against Barbara's friends and the amount of time Barbara spent with them.

"Well, first of all, I have no friends up here, and second of all, I'm not alone all day. I'm with Brucey a lot. And third, reading the classics is very educational! You said so once yourself. Think how happy Grandma would be if she knew I was finally reading those old books."

"Brucey is nine years old!!! You are fourteen. This is not normal."

"The Johnsons love that I entertain Brucey all day! And they're really nice about it. They often feed me lunch and sometimes take us out on the boat. Last year you told me it was really nice that I was helping them out with Brucey. Now suddenly I'm a freak for trying to do something nice. I just don't get it." She said no more that night.

The next day when I heard her car coming I shoved my book under the chair, grabbed the binoculars and ran down to the pier. Then I came waltzing up and told my mom I'd been boy watching all day and seen a bunch of cute ones. She didn't appreciate my humor, but had some "wonderful" news for me. It was quite obvious to me that my mother had been unloading on her friends all the details of her youngest daughter's embarrassing social maladies.

"Mrs. Cook has invited you to spend the day with Peggy tomorrow." Leave it to benevolent Mrs. Cook to come to the rescue and fix me.

"Peggy Cook! You want me to spend a whole day with her?"

"You've played junior golf with her a couple of times. She's the same age as you are and a really nice girl." On various occasions my mother had also described her as sweet, friendly, beautiful, well groomed, personable, intelligent, charismatic, etc. etc. etc. In other words, she was everything I wasn't. I wished my mom would just adopt her and send me to live with Brucey's grandparents.

"I know who she is. Yes, she's nice. She's also gorgeous, popular and a cheerleader! She doesn't want to spend the day with me!"

"You're not making any sense at all. You think just because she's a cheerleader that she wouldn't want to be with you? I know she'll be really nice to you and you'll have a good time." It was clear that my mother understood absolutely nothing about the teenage social strata.

"Mom, she's got loads of friends over at Cedar Point, and they're all probably as cute and popular as she is. I don't know anybody. I'll feel stupid and uncomfortable."

"Don't be silly. But you are right about one thing; there are a lot of kids there. Kids your age, I might add, and now you will be able to meet them."

"Mom, don't make me do this! Besides, who'll take Brucey swimming tomorrow?"

"He is not your responsibility!"

"But I promised him we'd go treasure hunting tomorrow. You want to make a liar out of me?"

"You'll just have to tell him 'No' for a change. Blame it on me if you must."

"Gosh, you treat me like I'm three years old and you're taking me to play with the other babies!"

"Well, if you weren't acting like a three year old, I wouldn't have to treat you like one." That comment sent me off to my room where I escaped into a Nancy Drew mystery. I refused to eat any dinner telling my mom I just wasn't hungry. She woke me up early the next morning and told me to get ready to go. I wished I'd run off during the night. I couldn't figure out what to wear. I had one nice pair of Bermuda shorts that I'd wear when I had to play golf, but all my blouses were stupid and babyish looking. I slipped into Barbara's room and woke her up apologetically.

"Barbara, you've got to help me out. Can I borrow your yellow blouse?"

"You woke me up to ask me that? Get out. There is no way! You'll just ruin it."

"Oh please! Mom is making me spend the day with Peggy Cook. I've got nothing to wear."

"Wear your Lakeview High T shirt. That'll be fine." At least they'd know I was in high school. I probably had the body of a ten year old; quite a contrast to Peggy, who looked to be about seventeen. I debated whether to bring my black Speedo or the yellow bikini that I'd wasted my money on the summer before. I settled on the Speedo, thinking maybe we'd have swimming races. Peggy was quite an athlete. I made my way down the stairs.

"Go back and comb your hair," my mother advised. I'd already tried, but I was too tired to argue with her so I went back and repeated the useless gesture. I was too upset to eat any breakfast. I climbed into the car and sat there speechless. My mother droned on about my lousy attitude and my lack of appreciation and how someday I'd thank her for this. I didn't hear most of it. I was just staring out at the woods and fields looking for places to bury treasure and wondering how running through them and exploring them had suddenly become a sick abnormality in my mother's eyes.

We drove through Cedar Point Park to a large white house where we were greeted by the ever cheerful and vivacious Mrs. Cook. She took me aside, held both my hands in hers and looked down at me with big concerned eyes. "And how are you, my dear?" It was the tone you might use with someone who'd just been let out of a mental institution. I just stared back with doleful eyes. I opened my mouth part way and froze in that posture. I think I managed to freak her out pretty good, I certainly was able to out stare her. "Well, never mind," she said nervously, "you're going to have such a wonderful day today." Fishing for something else to say she noticed my T shirt. "Oh, Lake View High! Yeah, Rah, Go Go Lakeview! I didn't realize you went to Lakeview."

"I don't. I found the shirt washed up on the shore of the lake," I said, in a dull monotone, "but I can't figure out what happened to the person inside."

"Oh. OK. Well, Peggy is just getting up, but she'll be down right away." She introduced me to Peggy's old grandmother who owned the house and would be watching us all day. Then she and my mom took off for the country club. I wasn't sure just exactly what to do with myself. I played with the cat for a while. I sat on the couch and looked at magazines until Granny sat in the big easy chair and turned on the TV at full volume. I couldn't believe Peggy could sleep through the noise. We watched some stupid game shows. Great way to spend the summer, I thought.

Eventually Peggy made her way down the stairs, dressed in pink striped pajamas with her hair up in rollers. "Oh my gosh!" she said. "I forgot you were coming! Oh, I look horrid, I'm so embarrassed."

"It's OK," I said. Actually she still looked gorgeous, but I was delighted to catch her in a moment of awkwardness. I hadn't imagined it ever happened to someone like her.

"Have you been here long? You should've gotten me up. Hey, do you want a bowl of Lucky Charms?"

"No thanks," I answered, still way too nervous to eat.

She went over and gave Granny a great big kiss, and walked into the kitchen. A moment later she came out with a bowl of cereal. She tucked her legs up under herself and sat down on the couch beside me. "You have to forgive the volume of the TV. Granny can't hear very well. So, what do you want to do today?"

"I don't care," I answered, not because I didn't, but because I didn't have a clue about what exactly to do with someone like Peggy.

After she finished her cereal she invited me up to her room. She put on a Beatles record and she sang along with it as she transformed herself into Miss America. She swapped out the pink flannel pajamas for a pair of very short shorts and a sexy top that she filled out perfectly. She pulled out the rollers and fussed with every strand of hair until she looked like she was ready to go to a prom. She asked me, "Are you still going over to junior golf? I managed to get out of it last week by pretending to be sick."

"But I thought you liked it. You're so good at it."

"Are you kidding? I only go because my mom makes me."

"Me too! I really hate it."

"Keep your eye on the ball, eye on the ball," she said in a deep raspy voice, perfectly imitating the pro who gave the lessons. She went on mimicking all his lines until she had me laughing hysterically. "And that conceited son of his, Robert, I just can't stand him." Peggy added.

"I know, all I ever hear is how good he is and at such a young age, and how I could get to be as good as him."

"Yeah, I know," she said. "As if I would actually want to be. Have you ever played golf with him?"

"Oh no, I'm terrible at golf. There's no kind of way I'd play with him."

"Well, my mom made me play with him! All he did the whole time was tell me how good he was and point out everything I was doing wrong."

"Why do moms do stuff like that?" I asked, knowing full that Peggy was also being forced into spending a day with me. I wondered what she'd be telling her friends about me.

"I don't know. I think my mom thinks I'm three years old sometimes. I'm so glad she's on the golf course most of the summer, otherwise I'd really go nuts."

"Yeah," I answered. "I know exactly what you mean."

While we talked, Peggy was putting on her make-up, transforming her already pretty face into a work of art. I tried not to gawk. "How come you don't wear make-up?" she asked.

"I wear a little at school, but I don't bother with it when I'm up here."

"Maybe you should. You're not really ugly, you know." I wasn't quite sure how to take that. "I bet you'd look really nice in make-up. Hey, can I do up your face? I'm really good at it. I'm thinking about becoming a beauty consultant after high school. Of course, my parents are 'sickened at the very thought of it.' They want me to go to Northwestern."

"Oh my gosh, that's where my dad wants me to go!"

Just then there was a loud knock on the bedroom door. "Bonnie, is that you? Come on in." Peggy yelled. Another beautiful teen-aged specimen walked through the door, just as dolled up as Peggy. "Hey Bonnie, this is my friend, Sandy." Friend? She called me friend? "Our mothers play on the golf team together."

"Oh, this is the one . . ." Bonnie cut herself off immediately. "I thought she was coming next week. Well, I can come back tomorrow."

"No, no, don't go!" Peggy said frantically. "Sandy would love for you to hang out with us, right Sandy?" She smiled at me and turned to Bonnie with pleading eyes.

"Well, OK. I'll stay." Peggy was tall and thin with pretty blonde hair worn in a flip. She had big brown eyes, sort of like Bambi's, and a sweet endearing smile. We made small talk, like about where we were from and where we went to school and stuff like that. The Beatles still filled in the background. Bonnie joined Peggy in singing, "Oh she was just seventeen . . ."

After it was over, Bonnie swooned. "I can so clearly see Paul's adorable face when I hear that song. He is sooooo cute."

"Yeah, but Dennis McPhearson is every bit as cute! And he lives right here and doesn't have every girl in the whole world after him." Peggy added.

"Only every girl in Walworth County," Bonnie said dejectedly.

"Come on, let's go," said Peggy. They both took a good long look in the full- length mirror, satisfied at what they saw. Then they looked at me and exchanged embarrassed glances.

"Hey," said Peggy, "I've got an old blouse that I just love, but it doesn't fit me anymore. You'd look great in it. She pulled out a frilly pink blouse. It was so pink. It just shouted out cuteness and girliness. I tried it on and we all three examined me in the mirror.

Bonnie grabbed a bunch of tissues and handed them to me. "Here, this'll help."

"Huh?" I looked up at her, confused.

"You know," she said, pointing down at my non-existent breasts.

"No, I'll feel stupid, and they'll probably fall out."

She shrugged and lay them all on the bed. "Hey, let me do your hair! I'm gonna be a cosmetologist!"

Peggy chimed in, "Yeah, we're going into business together after high school. Bonnie's gonna do the hair, and I'm gonna do the make-up."

"That's great," I said. "I'll bet you'll have a really successful business! But I don't want my hair done." They just looked at each other and rolled their eyes.

"Well, let's just go," Peggy said. I didn't ask where we were going, just followed along. We got downstairs and Peggy approached her grandmother. "Grammy," she yelled over the blaring TV, "do you need me to get some cream for your coffee?"

"Oh, yes, dear, that would be so kind of you. Your mother always forgets to buy it. Go get me my purse." With that Grammy pulled out a few dollars and handed them to Peggy. "Here, and a little extra, so you can buy some ice cream treats for your friends." She smiled at us for the first and only time that day.

"Oh thanks, Grammy!" Peggy gave her a big hug and kiss. Bonnie and I thanked her too, and the three of us were off to Bell's Grocery Store and Bait Shop. I'd been there plenty of times with my mom. We started walking in the opposite direction.

"Isn't Bells that way?" I asked timidly, pointing up the hill.

"We have to go by Dennis McPhearson's house first." After we walked a long way in the opposite direction Peggy pointed, "There, see the brown house with the awning? No, don't stare! Just walk by like you don't know." So we walked by trying to appear natural and casual, though I couldn't help but notice Peggy's hips swaying a bit more, and Bonnie flipping her hair. We walked to the end of the street, turned around and walked past it again.

"I wonder what he's doing," Bonnie said.

"He's probably still sleeping," Peggy said. "I bet he was out late, probably dancing at Majestic. Sandy, you wouldn't believe what a fabulous dancer he is!"

"Sometimes he has to work for his dad. His dad owns McPhearson's air conditioning in Elkhorn." Bonnie added. "Or, maybe he's practicing football or something. Ya know he plays varsity football and basketball at Williams Bay High, and he's only a sophomore. He's like the perfect specimen of mankind."

"He lives here year around? Lucky him." I said. "Doesn't he have a girlfriend?"

"That's just it," Bonnie said. "They just broke up. I mean, like a couple of days ago. That's why I've got to see him now."

"As you can see," Peggy said, "Bonnie is hopelessly in love with him. The guys up here always go for the summer girls so there's hope. Of course I'm kind of crazy about him myself, which presents sort of a problem."

"I thought you were going steady?" I said.

"Well, yeah, but he's back in Oak Park. I'm here!" We continued on to Bell's and Peggy called out, "Hi, Sam, my grandmother needs some cigarettes."

"Oh, hey there, Peggy, and how is your grandma today?"

"OK, I guess. She just can't get around very well anymore."

"Yeah, well, that's what happens when people get old. Salems, right? Say 'Hi' to her from Sam, OK?"

"Sure thing, bye bye!" We walked out with neither cream nor ice cream treats, only the pack of Salems.

I didn't know whether she would appreciate a reminder or not, but I finally said, "You forgot the cream."

She laughed. "My grandmother doesn't really need any cream. But she forgets every day. This is how we get our cigarette money." When I was little, my grandma walked up here every morning for cigarettes with me in tow. I'm just continuing the tradition. We walked back down, passing Dennis McPhearson's house a third and then a fourth time. Then we turned up a different road, crossed a little stone bridge, and ambled down to a dry creek bed. Brucey would have loved the place. There, hidden by the bridge, Peggy and Bonnie lit up.

"Here, you want one," Peggy offered.

"No, thanks," I replied.

"You don't smoke, do ya?" Bonnie asked. I shook my head.

"That's OK," Peggy said. "Here, just try a puff of mine." Naturally I tried it and ended up coughing my head off. Bonnie tried to cover her laughter but wasn't able to. "That's always how it is the first time," Peggy said, consolingly. "You'll get used to it. Let me know when you want another puff."

"Do you ever go to Majestic?" Bonnie asked.

"No, I don't know how to dance. I suppose you go there all the time."

"Whenever we can get a ride. It's really great most of the time, but there's gotten to be some weird kids over there."

Peggy chimed in, "Oh yeah, like 'Miss Big Nose'. She's so conceited! She wears the ugliest, most garish colors and they always clash! She must be colorblind."

"She's the worst dancer! It's like she's *trying* to look goofy!" Bonnie started jerking her body around like she was having a seizure. Peggy laughed.

"Then there's 'Miss Skin Tight'. You can see *everything,* and I do mean *everything!* She dances so dirty! I can't believe they don't kick her out."

"Her hair is teased and stands about a foot off her head."

"I'm sure there's got to be cockroaches living inside."

"She always dances with those spics from Chicago. They *love* the way she dances!"

"I think they're hoping she'll comb her fingers through they're greasy hair!"

"Oh, I'm sure she has, and a lot worse too!"

"I hate greasers!"

"Yeah, they're always starting fights."

"Oh, did you see that fat girl, the one from Delavan, kissing John Newton? Oh, now, *that* was disgusting!"

"No, I missed it, I was too busy watching Mary Kelly trying to get Peter to notice her. What an idiot she is."

The conversation continued like this while they smoked a couple of cigarettes. I could only imagine what they'd be saying about me the next day!

Finally we climbed out of the creek bed and walked, guess where, past Dennis McPhearson's house for the fifth and sixth times. Although I was relieved that the girls were being relatively nice to me, the ridiculousness of this situation was wearing on me. Besides, I was getting hungry. I judged it to be around one or two o'clock, way past lunchtime. I imagined Grammy probably had some huge lunch prepared for us; hot dogs, hamburgers or sandwiches. I didn't care what, anything would taste good to my growling stomach. I was eager to get back to the house.

Just then we saw a tall red headed guy coming down the steps of a house up the street. "That's Trevor, Dennis's best friend," Bonnie whispered. "He's a great basketball player." Then she called out to him, "Hey, Trevor! Trevor!"

He came toward us with a huge smile on his face. "Oh, Bonnie, hey!" he said, as his eyes scanned her from head to toe "Uh," his face was turning a little red, "Uh, hi, Peggy. Where are you girls going?"

Bonnie answered quickly, "Just kind of hanging out. What are you guys up to today?"

"I think we're going skiing, but I've got to talk to Dennis."

"That sounds really fun, ask him if we can go with," Peggy said. Bonnie shot her an excited glance. The four of us went traipsing back to Dennis's house. We girls waited on the street. Evidently Dennis's mother didn't take kindly to girls googling at his door. I was excited about water skiing. Maybe my mom had been right. Skiing with a bunch of friends would be great, especially because I was a great skier. I'd make a good impression. Then I began stressing about the suit I'd brought. My tank suit was far better for skiing, but the bikini would've looked sexier and more grown up. After about fifteen minutes Trevor came back out, and behind him followed the legendary Dennis McPhearson in his bathing suit. He was tall and muscular in all the right places. He had dark brown, almost black hair, and deep, dreamy, warm eyes. OH MY GOD! I was mesmerized by those eyes. The entire ridiculous morning suddenly made sense to me. Somehow through the mystical fog I heard Peggy say, "And this is Sandy. Sandy loves to water ski, right?"

Oh my god, he was looking at me. They were expecting me to actually answer something. "Yeah," I said, and smiled the best smile I knew how to do. The

boys told us to put on our suits and meet them down at the pier. Our conversation on the way back to the house consisted mostly of "oohs," "aahs," "wows," and a bunch of complimentary descriptive words, none of which came close to describing Dennis McPhearson in the flesh.

When we arrived back at Peggy's house, Grammy was sound asleep in front of a blaring soap opera. No lunch, as I'd hoped, but the excitement of water skiing helped me to forget about my gnawing stomach. Bonnie ran home to get her suit, and Peggy and I ran up to her bedroom. She tried on three different bikinis trying to figure out which one she looked best in. She touched up her make-up and then looked down at noodle shaped me stuck in my black tank suit. "You don't by chance have a bathing suit you've outgrown, do you?" I asked.

"No, but, here, just cover up with this." She handed me a cute little baby blue beach dress.

We picked Bonnie up at her house and walked down to the lake path, and over to the pier where Trevor's dad's boat was. Sitting against a tree on shore there was a girl about our age reading. Peggy yelled out in her sweet, miss popularity voice, "Hi, Betsy, what ya reading? Nice to see you." We walked out to the end of the pier, hopefully out of earshot. "That's Betsy the Bookworm. I swear, that kid always has her nose in a book."

Bonnie replied, "Well, if I were that ugly, I'd keep my nose in a book all the time too!"

"Hey, I heard her parents are getting a divorce."

"Oh, I wonder which one of them's gonna get stuck with her!" As we waited for what felt like hours, they continued to gossip. I wanted to go swimming, but only little kids were in the water, and it was obvious Bonnie and Peggy didn't want their hair messed up before the boys came down.

Finally we saw Trevor trotting toward us, breathing hard. "I'm sorry, we can't go skiing; I can't find the boat key. I don't know what happened to it. I looked everywhere." Bonnie shook her head and gave him a "you moron" kind of stare. Peggy shrugged her shoulders. I was really disappointed. Trevor looked like a puppy that had just been beaten. "B-b-but, hey," he stammered, "does anybody want to swim out to the raft with me?"

"I do!" Then I felt foolish, not cool at all. The invitation had been meant for Bonnie, exclusively. He never took his eyes off of her once during his whole sorry delivery.

"Where's Dennis?" she asked.

"His mom's making him cut the lawn, but he said it'll only take him about an hour."

"Why don't you guys come over to my house when he's done?" Peggy offered.

"Yeah, OK," Trevor said, with a huge smile, scanning Bonnie again. I wondered how it would feel to have a guy look at *me* like that. I wasn't sure whether or not I'd like it, but it wasn't an issue because I knew it would never happen.

"You will come, right? And bring Dennis!" On the way back up to the house Bonnie asked, "Do you think they'll actually come?"

Peggy answered, "Trevor will be there for sure, he's really got a thing for you!"

Bonnie groaned, "Yuck! I think he's so gawky and homely. But, he is Dennis's best friend. It's the only way we'll ever get close to Dennis."

Then Peggy asked, "Hey, Bonnie, will you do my nails? They're all chipped."

"Sure, I've got that new color, light salmon berry. It's really nice. Maybe you can do mine too. Do you think Dennis really had to cut the lawn?"

"Well, there's one sure way to find out! Sandy, do you remember where Dennis's house is?" How could I not, after walking past it some eight times. "Why don't you go up and see if he's really cutting the lawn. His mother's gonna get really mad if she sees us again, but she doesn't know you. Besides, if just one person walks by he's less likely to notice. We don't want him to think we're desperate or anything."

Naturally I agreed. As I approached his house I heard the sound of a lawn mower. There he was, mowing the lawn, still shirtless. I watched for a while, drooling, even though I knew a guy like Dennis would never be interested in a girl like me. As I was standing there, he suddenly caught sight of me. He continued to mow, but gave me a quick smile and a wave. It sent a strange and euphoric feeling through my body. One I'd never experienced before. Oh my goodness, I thought, maybe, just maybe, he likes me. I floated back down to Peggy's house about three feet off the ground. I crept past the sleeping grandmother and on up to Peggy's room where the Beatles were still singing. I was delighted to report that Dennis was, indeed, cutting the lawn.

"He didn't see you, did he?" Peggy asked.

"No, of course not," I lied.

The girls had slipped out of their suits and I did the same. I put the frilly little pink top back on, then went over to the bed and grabbed the tissue Bonnie had left there. I stuffed. I was looking better. "Bonnie, do you still want to do my hair?"

"OK, but we'll have to hurry, the guys might actually show up here soon." She pulled it up into a kind of a donut thing and teased it and pinned it until it all sat on top of my head looking smart and sophisticated. She doused it all in hair spray. I was uncomfortable not having my hair to hide behind, but in the mirror I saw a girl who actually looked to be fourteen. Then I looked at Peggy.

"You want me to do your make-up?" she asked. When she was done I looked into the mirror again and was extremely pleased with what stared back.

"Thanks, I like it," I said.

"You look really good," Peggy said. "You should wear make-up all the time."

Bonnie was also full of compliments. I was so ready for the guys to come. We went down and sat on the screened porch waiting. After a long while we saw them walking up the street; Dennis was still shirtless. We met them on the front steps where we talked for a while. Or, rather, they all talked for a while. I simply had nothing cool to say. I would just kind of giggle along at all the places where they giggled, kind of like the laugh track of a bad sit com. I sat there kind of wanting to be noticed, but hoping, on the other hand, that I wouldn't be.

"Hey, are you guys thirsty? Do you want some pop?" Peggy asked.

"You got anything a little stronger?" Dennis asked, with his million dollar smile.

"Sure," Peggy answered, as a big mischievous smile spread across her face. "But we can't drink it out here. Just wait a sec." When she came back out she said, "Come on, we can go up to my room. Bonnie, show them where it is. I'll make sure my grandma doesn't see you." With that we all tiptoed through the living room, as if our footsteps could possibly be heard above the still blaring TV set. We made it safely to Peggy's room where Bonnie immediately put the Beatles back on. Peggy entered with a couple of bottles of beer. We sat on the floor together and began passing the first bottle around. I'd always liked the taste of beer, so this was easy for me. They were very generous with me, encouraging me to take a few extra gulps to every one of theirs. As the bottle circulated and the conversation got funnier and funnier, I finally began to feel like a part of the group. I even said one or two things that made everyone else laugh. After I guzzled down the last of the second bottle I began spinning it on the floor.

"Hey," I ventured to ask, "Does anyone want to play spin the bottle?" They all looked at me a little surprised, but agreed.

"You go first," they all said. I spun and it landed on Bonnie.

"Do over!" she protested. "Girls shouldn't have to kiss girls."

"No do-overs, that's the game," Dennis insisted. I gave Bonnie a quick peck on the cheek. She groaned and wiped it off with a tissue.

"Peggy, I think I'm gonna need more beer if we're gonna continue this game," Bonnie said. We all agreed. This sent Peggy down for some more bottles, which were passed around as we continued to play.

Then it was Trevor's turn. He got to kiss Peggy, though I knew he really wanted to be kissing Bonnie. Bonnie was next and she also got Peggy. "Gross," she complained, "this is a stupid game. Give me another swig."

Then it was Dennis's turn. I crossed my fingers and wished on my lucky star and everything else I knew to do, and it worked. It landed on me. I was to be kissed by Dennis. He was moving toward me; my heart was flipping over. But before he reached me we heard a car door slam evoking a loud gasp from Peggy. She ran to the open window, "*Oh my god*, my mom's home already! She'll kill me if she finds guys up here. Hide in the closet!"

"But my kiss," I yelled. "First I get my kiss."

"Oh stop," Peggy pleaded, "we've got to hide them."

"For how long?" Dennis asked.

"I don't know. Just trust me." Trevor climbed into the little closet clumsily and noisily. Bonnie began laughing hysterically. I reached out and grabbed Dennis's arm.

"Let go!" Peggy screamed.

"You shouldn't have let her drink so much," Bonnie said, still laughing.

"I'm fine," I insisted. I just want my kiss!" I clung to Dennis. He turned around, looked at me and laughed.

"It's OK. I can take care of this," Dennis said confidently. Then he put his hand behind my head. He covered my mouth with his and gave me a great big long smooch. Then he smiled at me with those incredible eyes and scrambled into the closet, slamming the door behind him. Peggy and Bonnie just stared at me. They were both really angry. I swooned and fell onto the bed laughing. Peggy suddenly kicked back into action, hiding the beer bottles under her mattress and handing out peppermints.

'Suck on these! It'll get rid of the beer smell."

"And wash away the taste of Dennis's kiss? No way!" I continued giggling.

'Do something with her!' she yelled to Bonnie. "I'll go down and stall our moms."

"Do what? What am I supposed to do?"

"I'm fine," I told Bonnie. "You don't think that little bit of beer's 'nough to make me tipsy, do ya? I'm just high on Dennis's kiss. OOOOHHHHH," She scowled at me.

"It was a really stupid, juvenile game ya know!" Then she whispered, "Don't begin thinking that Dennis likes you or anything. He just kissed you because he had to and he feels sorry for you, just like everybody else does."

After Dennis's kiss, I was feeling way too good to let her words upset me. "Sure was nice though!" I

insisted. I walked down the stairs in rhythm to my
own resounding rendition of *I Want to Hold Your
Hand*. I wanted Dennis to hear it over the blasting
TV. No small feat, complicated by a staircase that had
suddenly gone all wobbly. I waltzed into the kitchen
where Peggy was talking to our moms.

"Hi Mommy!" I said, a bit too loudly. With one
hand on my hip and one on the back of my head,
I swayed my hips, and strutted my new look. How
d'you guys like it, huh? Ugly duckling turns swan."
Then I opened my mouth and hissed like the swan
in Lincoln Park Zoo had done the preceding winter.
"What 'chya think? Whoopsy!" I giggled as the tissues
fell out of my blouse. I picked them up, flapped them
and declared, "Swan returns to ugly duckling, quack
quack." My mom just stood there dumbfounded. "And
how the hell are YOU, Mrs. Cookie?"

"Sandy!" my mother gasped.

"Thank-you for a simply divine day! Your daughter is a magna, magnam, uhh, magnaminous, I mean
magnanimous host. Thank you for setting up this
playdate for Peggy and me." Peggy stood beside her
mom, speechless, her pretty face all scrunched up
with anxiety. Bonnie, standing behind me, let out a
loud burp. I began to giggle again and couldn't stop.

"Bonnie, are you OK?" Peggy's mom asked. "You
look white as a ghost!"

"I think maybe I'm coming down with the flu,"
she said. "I just need to go home."

"Peggy, walk her home, I'm worried about her."

"OK, Mom. Bye Sandy, it was nice having you."

"Bye Peggy-O, thanks for the frilly blouse and everything. I had a sssimply sssmashingly, sssplendidly sssuper time." I returned to my rousing rendition of *I Want to Hold Your Hand* as my mom steered me to the car.

On the way home my mother yelled at me for a while. I don't remember all that she said, but mostly it was about how embarrassed she was, and what a terrible time she would have facing Mrs. Cook again. As her own steam was beginning to run out, she finally asked me what we did all day. "We walked past Dennis McPhearson's house eight times, Mom, until we finally saw him, and oh my god, what a hunk. I'm so crazy about him. You can't believe how adorable he is. And his body! His muscles. Oh my god. He just makes me shiver all over, just looking at him. I will dream of kissing him all night long. I mean he is cuter than any TV star I've ever seen. God, I just love him!" I prattled on like that for a while, but fell asleep before we got home. I never did find out how he and Trevor got out of the closet.

My mother never said another word about my new look or my strange behavior. But, a couple of days later when she found me curled up in my favorite chair reading, a big smile crossed her face. "I've got a surprise for you." What now, I thought. "Look, my friend Mildred gave me several old books. Here's

a copy of *Captains Courageous*. I think this is a story
Brucey might like.

"Thanks Mom."

9

Sailing School

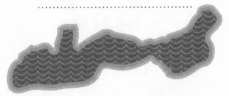

ꟼ'd planned on spending my fifteenth summer sleeping in every morning and lying in the hammock, immersed in my favorite authors every afternoon. As usual, my mother had other ideas. "How'd you like to take sailing lessons?" she asked, after spending the day with her new golfing buddy, Louise Barstow. I knew it was another of her attempts to socialize me, so I refused to make it easy on her.

"Let me think about it."

"Well, don't think about it too long, because the class will fill up. Louise's daughters are already signed up, and there's a space left for you if you want. Classes are held over at the yacht club. I think it would be loads of fun." At least she wasn't asking me to take more golf lessons, or hair fixing lessons, or anything of a finishing school nature. I'd never even been on a sailboat, but I'd always longed to be. I walked down to the pier and looked down toward Fontana. Always there were a few sailboats visible, and this evening was no exception. Sailboats dotted the lake, gliding by like graceful swans. Was it possible that I could actually learn to sail? Suddenly I was ecstatic at the prospect and darted back up the hill, but I approached my mother coolly and cautiously.

"So, how many classes are there? How will I get there? And, how old are Louise's daughters?" The classes would be held twice a week all summer long, Mom and Mrs. Barstow would take turns driving us over there, and Linda and Lettie were aged fourteen and ten. "Yeah, OK, I guess," I agreed, unenthusiastically, not wanting to give her too much satisfaction. Two days later I met Linda, who I got on very well with, and her clumsy little sister Lettie. Their mom drove us over to the yacht club.

There were twelve kids in the class, mostly ten year olds, but a few older kids, like Linda and me. During that first class we met our instructor, Gail, and her assistant, Marty, two college students who were not all that much older than me. We went around the circle saying our names, where we lived, and how much sailing experience we had. The amount of experience varied, from me, "I used to sail my toy boat tied to a string; I've watched some great movies about sailing the south-seas; and I've watched a whole lot of sailboats on the lake." I didn't actually say that though. "None," was my concise and honest answer. Linda and Lettie had been on a sailboat two or three times with their neighbors. Most of the rest sailed regularly with their families and had some crewing experience in races. Then there was Bobby Sales, to whom I took an instant disliking.

"I've crewed hundreds of times in races here on Lake Geneva, in all classes. I've also raced with my brother on Lake Michigan and with my dad down in the Bahamas, and a few times with my Grandpa down in the Florida Keys. Bobby was all of ten.

We were placed into groups, based on who we were sitting with, which put all the inexperienced ones, Linda, Lettie and me, in the same boat. Bobby and his experienced little friends were also together. We sat through a lecture on the parts of the boat and all its riggings. Gail had a big picture and a pointer. She quickly went over all the terms, and then had the class repeat it all back to her, in unison, as she pointed. Everyone seemed to know all the terms. I just faked it until she started pointing and asking individuals to identify the parts. When she got to me she pointed to a rope, "And this?" she asked.

"Um, uh, the halyard?" obviously wrong due to her dower expression. "I mean, the mainstay."

"Duh!" said Bobby, as a few others snickered.

"Tell her class, what is this?"

"The painter!" they all shouted in proud unison. My ego was bruised, needless to say, but I was eager to learn to sail. After another brief lecture on sailing basics, Gail handed out our sailing manuals. Much to my delight, the diagram was there. I determined I would learn all the names of all the riggings and other sailing terms. Mrs. Barstow was late picking us up. She'd slipped over to Big Foot Country Club to hit some practice balls. We sat on the big porch of the yacht club pouring over our books. I went inside to use the bathroom and caught sight of Gail out back making googley eyes with a tall, good looking blonde guy. I walked over to an open window to eavesdrop on their conversation.

"Are you nervous about your big race on Saturday?" she asked him.

"Maybe a little, but hey, I got a great boat and a great crew, we should be fine. How'd your first day of class go?"

"Good! I've got a few slow ones, but most of the kids already know a lot, so we should be able to get on the water next time."

"How'd my little brother do?"

"Bored out of his mind, of course," she laughed. Just then Bobby came flying around the corner.

"Hey Champ!" the tall blonde guy said. "How was sailing school?"

"Boring! I already know all that stuff. Why do I have to take it?"

"Cause Dad said! You know, I had to take it too! I think it really helps. Look, I'm a pretty good sailor, right?"

"Well, yeah! You win all the time!"

"Well, there ya go! You're gonna keep up the family tradition, right?" I found out later just how rich that family tradition was. Bobby's brother had won the Sheridan cup the year before, being the youngest ever to have done so. His father had won it numerous times before that, besides having competed in the World Cup more than once. His grandfather had competed in the Olympics and had been instrumental in establishing the Lake Geneva Yacht Club. He was quite a heroic figure around there.

Gail promised Bobby that, weather permitting, we'd be on the water next time and that it would be much more fun. I couldn't wait to start sailing.

Mrs. Barstow apologized for picking us up an hour late, but I didn't mind as we'd used the time to study over the sailing terminology. Lettie proudly handed her mom the sailing manual. Mrs. Barstow began pouring through it. "Oh, this looks good! It's a lot to learn!"

"Everybody else knows it all already!" Linda complained, echoing my sentiments. "I feel so dumb!"

Mrs. Barstow put her arm around Linda's shoulder, "Don't worry about it, you can learn this! Look, let's stop at the library on the way home and get some of these books that are recommended here in your manual." So, on the way home, that's exactly what we did. We stopped at the library and she checked out a couple of books on beginning sailing and ordered a couple more. Then she took us to the Riviera for ice cream, which seemed to help us tremendously.

"Did you have fun?" my Mom asked after I got home. Fun wasn't exactly the word I had in mind.

"No. It's like school, except I'm the oldest and dumbest one there."

"Oh, that's not true! Stop being so dramatic!" I stuck my nose in my sailing manual the rest of the evening. The next day I walked along the shore path to the Barstow's house over at the Lake Geneva Manor. Linda, Lettie and I poured over the terminology together and complained fiercely about conceited little Bobby Sales, or Mr. BS as we were fond of calling him.

During the next class we learned to rig the boat. There were four beautiful cub boats tied to the posts of the long pier in front of the yacht club, all facing the wind, lined up like perfect little soldiers. They were brand new that year! I couldn't wait to get started. Each group was assigned a boat, and Linda and I eagerly jumped aboard, confident that we knew just what to do. Then there was Lettie. She was standing, frozen on the pier, terrified. We pulled the boat in and held it against the pier. I held the boat and Linda took her hand and tried to coax her on. Gail and Marty were concentrating on the other three crews who were working like well-oiled machines, each member knowing just what to do. Their sails were already flapping in the wind.

"Good job, Bobby!" I heard Gail yell as the first boat left the dock. There were a few adults hanging around.

"Way to go, champ!" they yelled at Bobby.

"You guys are next," Gail yelled to the next crew, and off they went. About this time she seemed to notice that we hadn't even managed to climb on board yet. "Let me get this last boat started, then I'll help you guys," she shouted toward us. So off went the third boat, everyone happily heading out to the lake. "Gosh, I need to get out there," she said to no one in particular. "Marty! Help these guys!" Then she jumped into her little Boston Whaler from which she could supervise the others. Marty ambled over to our boat.

"What's the trouble?" he asked. Lettie's standing there, crying her eyes out! Linda is holding her hand, verbally encouraging her, awkwardly balanced with one foot on the pier and one on the boat. I am standing in the boat hanging onto a post for dear life, attempting to keep the boat from rocking. And he asks, "What's the trouble?"

Marty hadn't ever worked with kids before and he was as useless as we were. Finally we just gave up. Linda got out of the boat and sat on the pier with Lettie. I let go of the post and stared longingly at the other boats. "Can't we just go without her?" I asked Marty.

"No, you've got to have all three of you, one for the tiller, one for the main sail and one for the jib."

"So, why can't you just come with me and Linda?"

Linda was incensed. "I can't just leave her behind!"

"So, do we get our money back or what?" I said, angrily. I tried to hold back, but I began to cry, too, thinking we'd spend the whole class sitting at the pier. It was contagious, because Linda also began to cry and attempted to make apologies and excuses for Lettie. Marty just walked away.

After another few minutes the crying had subsided and a stony silence replaced it. One of the women who'd been standing and watching came over to us and took Lettie aside. She walked her out to the end of the pier and talked with her. We couldn't hear a word of what she said, but she returned with a dry eyed, willing Lettie. Once again we pulled the boat alongside the pier. Both Marty and Linda took a hand, and with the encouragement of the kind lady, Lettie stepped on board. We didn't ask her to do any of the rigging. We just sat her up by the jib, which she was to manage. Under Marty's tutelage we stuck in the battens, pulled up the jib, hoisted the mainsail, adjusted the tiller and lowered the centerboard. We checked all the ropes and Linda pushed off. I had the tiller, and finally we were headed out!

It was absolutely glorious! After all those years of dreaming, I was actually sailing a boat. I felt like I was flying. We finally got out to where the other boats were, just going back and forth. My proud reverie was disrupted as Bobby yelled out, "Man, what happened to you guys?" His crewmembers laughed.

"Oh, you wouldn't understand, C-H-A-M-P!" I said, drawing out the champ sarcastically.

We came about successfully a couple of times. Lettie managed to move awkwardly from one side to the other, much to my relief. Before I knew it, Gail was telling us it was time to go in. She insisted that our boat go in first, assuming we would have the most difficulty landing. I protested that it wasn't fair since we got out so late, but she'd hear none of it. The wind was steady and straight out of the west, so I was confident I could land the boat perfectly. I glided in on a beam reach, parallel to the pier, and just as we reached our post, I turned the boat into the wind. It was supposed to come to a nice stop, facing the wind. The sail was supposed to luff, and one of my crew members was supposed to catch the post and tie up the boat. That was how the demonstration had gone! Instead, I came about, but picked up speed. I crashed, hard, against the post. The loud thud and Lettie's scream caught everyone's attention. The boat bounced back and then we were stuck in irons, facing the wind, unable to control the boat, just drifting backwards. Marty shouted at us to push out the main sail. Just before we hit the rocks, the wind caught us and we were heading back out to the lake. "Go out and try it again! Watch your tell-tale!" On my second try I realized I had misjudged the direction of the wind. This time I turned the boat and headed it to the northwest. This time it worked. Linda failed to catch the pier, but she did manage to throw Marty the rope. He tied us up and we began letting down the sails.

In the meantime, the other boats drifted in. I watched as they each executed perfect landings. Not a single one messed up like I had! They all seemed to lower the sails and unrig their boats quickly and efficiently. They couldn't help but notice our bungling and boggling as we struggled to do the same. Neither did they fail to notice the damage I'd done to the chrome rail on the front of the boat.

"Hey, you guys," Bobby yelled to his friends, "look at the bow of their boat! Look what they did!"

"Oh man, look at that boat!"

"Brand new boat! Nice play Shakespeare!" Gail was none too pleased either, and just shook her head when she saw it.

I didn't tell my mom, who picked us up and greeted us with her usual, "Did you have fun?"

On the days there was no sailing school, I continued to review and practically memorize our manual. Linda let me take home the library books for a few days so I could read them more intensely. We got together a few times to study, to complain about Bobby, and to practice tying knots. On the bowline the little rabbit was supposed to come out of a hole and around the tree and back into the hole. I could never figure out which one was the tree, but Lettie was actually very good at it, and helped us. We learned to splice rope too. I redid all the lines on my Dad's speedboat, but he didn't much appreciate it.

Our second time on the boat was better. Lettie had to go sit on the end of the pier for a few minutes before boarding, a ritual she never quit doing. I was totally annoyed, but nobody else seemed to care. We were still the last boat out, but the rigging had gone much quicker than the first time, with almost no help from Marty. Linda was skipper and handled the boat just fine. We had to have a man overboard drill. It took us three tries to pick up the alleged man, but we finally got him. I thought we did well, but Gail promised that our man would have been long dead before we got there. The other kids appreciated her humor, Bobby especially. I certainly did not.

Everyone had to take turns as skipper, and so on our third time out Lettie took the tiller. It was a bad day for that because the wind was gusting, sometimes out of the north and sometimes out of the west. We pushed off and started on a close reach, but the wind kept shifting forcing her to compensate. The boat was headed straight for a beautiful wooden Chris Craft tied on a buoy. "Come about! Come about!" I yelled. "Turn around! Turn around!"

"Push the handle away from you! Quick!" yelled Linda. But Lettie panicked. I had the jib so I climbed up front and tried to reduce the impact. Maybe I did, but we left a good scratch on the beautifully finished boat. My pushing off caused us to come about, startling Lettie, who screamed as the sail swung over, barely missing her head. Linda managed to calm her down, coaxing her to move to the high side of the boat and stay on a high reach, sailing safely away from the boat we'd just hit. Unfortunately our transgression was clearly seen by Gail, who gave us a good tongue lashing and told us that we, our whole crew, was responsible for the boat damage and she'd be calling the owner and our parents and blah, blah, blah. All this as poor Lettie, already shaking in fear, was trying to keep the boat sailing. Gail rode along side of us for a little while. She instructed Lettie to come about again. Lettie went part way, got scared, and landed us in irons, stopped dead, headed straight into the wind. Gail was visibly frustrated with us, but coached us out of it. After a few more tries, Lettie was catching on to the coming about thing. Just as I was beginning to relax, one of the tour boats passed by. It was nowhere near us, but Lettie was sure we were going to hit it. She changed directions, but she jibed instead of coming about. The mainsail swung over violently, nearly decapitating all three of us, and nearly dumping us over. After that, Gail ordered us off the lake.

"It's just too windy for you guys!"

With Linda's help, Lettie managed to land the boat with only a small thud, adding no further damage to the boat. Sadly we unrigged everything and just sat on the end of the pier watching the others. Juicy gossip spread fast, and as each of the crews landed we heard a barrage of comments. "You guys hit that boat!"

"Oh my god, that guy's gonna be SO mad!"

"I know the owner of that boat, boy, are you guys in trouble!"

The worst came from the champ, of course, "I can't believe you can't sail in this wind! It's hardly windy at all!" Parents were already hanging around the pier, ready to drive home their darlings, full of encouraging words and loving smiles. One old man caught my attention. He looked kind of like a dignified version of Popeye, complete with a long gray beard, a pipe and sailor cap. He seemed to commandeer everyone's respect.

"How're ya doin' Cap?"

"Hey Cap!"

"Nice to see you, Cap!" Some of the kids walked up to him and shook his hand.

"Grandpa!" shouted Bobby, who ran up to him and gave him a big hug.

"Hey, Champ! You did a great job out there today! I've been watching you!"

"Let's just walk out to the road and meet my mom there, OK?" I asked the girls. Gladly they followed me as we walked off the pier, heads down, wishing we were the recipients of some nice words too, yet hoping, at the same time, not be noticed.

My mom was late, like always. We stood up on the road trying to figure out how we were going to pay for the boat damage. When she finally got there, she was all cheery and excited. "Hi girls. Did you have fun?" None of us said anything. She seemed not to notice, but chattered on about some big deal going on at the country club. Why couldn't she be like the other parents?

Over the next few days we were all tense, anticipating the phone call from Gail or the angry boat owner,
but it never came. I was really scared to go back to sailing school, and seriously thought about quitting. I even
talked to Linda and Lettie about it. They felt the same,
but their mother wouldn't let them quit. I thought my
mom might actually enjoy not having to take her turn
driving, but the lessons had already been paid for, so
I'm not sure she'd have let me quit anyway. But, I never
got around to asking her, because the girls begged me
to hang in there with them, and I felt a sense of loyalty.
"You wouldn't let us face Mr. BS all by ourselves, would
you?" Linda pleaded. I couldn't let them down.

We didn't go out on the lake the following class
because we had to have a written test. I had all the confidence in the world that I could ace it. I'd done so much
reading and studying, and besides, I was already in high
school, whereas most everyone else was in fifth or sixth
grade. The test seemed easy and I finished it quickly.
As we finished, Marty and Gail would test us individu-
ally on our knot tying, while parent volunteers graded
our tests. They returned our graded tests to us immediately and I was devastated that I'd gotten three wrong!
Naturally I had to look around and compare scores with
everyone else. "Oh, you got 100," I said to Bobby.

"Well, duh, yeah, of course! What'd you expect?"
Well, excuse me, Mr. BS. I was so mad at him. I
HATED him, conceited little punk!

I looked over my test carefully. There was one where I just misunderstood the question, one I really didn't know, but a third one where I was just sure I was right. I approached Gail, "I don't understand. Look at this question. Isn't it called a beam reach when you're going right perpendicular to the wind?"

"Yes, you're right.

"But it's marked wrong!" I protested.

"OK! The volunteer just made a mistake; don't be so upset!" She corrected it on my test and in the grading book. Then she called in the other tests. It turned out they'd all been graded wrong, so most everyone got one more right, but Bobby got one wrong. Small victory, but I went home happy that day!

After that we began racing. By now we'd learned all the terminology, had done all the safety drills, had learned the racing and right-of-way rules, and had, more or less, learned to work together as a crew. The first race was predictable. Bobby's boat came in first by a long-shot, the next two were pretty close. We came trailing in, way behind everyone else, and finished lowering our sails long after everyone had gone home. Over the next few races, Bobby and his crew continued grabbing first place. Second and third place altered, and we continued to come in last. The gap, however, was closing just slightly. We started getting back to the pier before everyone else had left. Always there were a few parents and other sailing

enthusiasts who would make a big deal over everything, especially Bobby. "Hey Champ!"

"Way to go, Bobby!"

"Nice turn around that last buoy!"

"Next time, pull that jib just a tad tighter and you'll improve even more!"

"Great job guys!" Etc., etc. etc.

We had no cheerleaders, no welcoming committee. I guess it was just as well. What would they have said? "Hurray, last again! Congratulations on your consistency! Try again next time." We'd just unrig the boat and walk slowly up the road, to be picked up by our always-late mothers who neither knew nor cared one bit about sailing. "Did you have fun?" seemed to be the only thing they knew to ask. They were clueless.

Our main problem, besides our obvious lack of experience, was Lettie's fear. Both Linda and I were making some progress, keeping up close enough to the others that at least it looked like we were in the same race. That was as much as we hoped for. But, Lettie just kept doing stupid things, like letting the main sail luff if we got going too fast, and when she was skipper, it was always disastrous. At the start of a race, she was scared to go too close to the start line. She'd just hang back, put the boat in irons, and wait for all the other boats to cross. Then we'd have to do everything we could to get out of irons and get some momentum to cross the start line. As soon as we started to pick up speed, she'd get frightened and change tack slightly to try to slow us down. One time we were headed down wind on the last leg of the race when a motorboat approached. Lettie looked worried. "Don't worry, Lettie," I said, "We've got the right of way."

"Hold your course, Lettie," Gail shouted. "That boat will give you the right of way." Everyone else had finished by this time and I'm sure she was anxious to flirt with Bobby's brother, or to get home.

"Just hang in there, Lettie. You're doing great!" Linda said.

But Lettie wasn't buying any of this. She got scared and turned quickly away from the motorboat.

She never understood the difference between jibing and coming about. She just turned the boat, oblivious to the direction of the wind. Once again the sail came flying over the boat, but this time it took us with it. One minute we were sailing and the next thing I knew I was in the water, my arm was killing me. Gail was yelling out a bunch of things that didn't register on my stunned brain. I was trying to figure out what had happened, and whether my arm was broken. "Don't let it turtle! Don't let it turtle!" I finally heard her say. So, we'd capsized. I knew what we were supposed to do, and our training drove my instincts. I swam to the front of the boat to grab the painter, but Linda already had it, and was turning the boat into the wind. Gail was screaming at me to get over to the centerboard. Oh, yeah, OK. My life jacket was cumbersome and my arm hurt like the dickens, but somehow I managed to paddle around to the centerboard and climb onto it. I concluded that my arm wasn't broken, because I was able to grab the side of the boat. I pulled myself up and stood on the centerboard. I used my weight to right the boat, just like we'd practiced, but nothing happened. I wasn't strong enough or heavy enough, or maybe I just wasn't doing it right. During practice, two of us had pulled the boat up, I needed Lettie's weight.

"Lettie, get up here and help me!" I screamed, trying to overpower Gail's incessant barking. "Lettie! I need your help!" I was so mad at her. It was her stupidity that had caused all this, and now she wasn't even willing to help me. I yelled some more, restraining myself from using the choice words passing through my brain. She refused to answer me, and I was growing madder by the second, until I suddenly realized that I couldn't see her. Suddenly I panicked. "Oh my god, where's Lettie? Linda, where's Lettie? Lettie!!!" I screamed at the top of my voice. "Gail, stop screaming at me. We've got to find Lettie!" I was bawling by this time.

"Calm down!" Gail yelled back.

"Lettie's OK," Linda shouted. Just then I looked over and saw a motorboat, the same one that had frightened Lettie to begin with. It was only about twenty-five yards away, with a whole bunch of people on board. They were hanging their ladder over the side and helping a kid climb on board. I looked again. Sure enough, it was Lettie. Evidently she'd started swimming for shore and they picked her up. I was so happy and relieved that she was alright, but my anger soon washed out all the good feelings. She'd deserted us! You're never ever supposed to leave the boat!!! Meantime, Gail didn't come up for air. She continued to shout out orders, but try as I would, I just couldn't get the boat righted.

The motorboat drew slightly closer and suddenly a gorgeous, muscular guy yelled out, "You look like you need some help." He dove off the boat and swam right over to me. He joined me on the centerboard and with one pull we had the boat righted. He easily pulled himself in and then helped me and Linda back onto the boat. He was soooo cute! We thanked him over and over. Even Gail thanked him. She was clearly exasperated. "Will you be OK now?" he asked.

"Yeah, thanks again," Linda and I answered. They took Lettie back to the Yacht Club pier, while Linda and I sailed back. Gail, who must've had a sore throat by this time, finally was quiet. She motored back slowly. I dreaded getting back to the pier anticipating both Gail's lecture and the nasty jeers of our classmates, but none of that happened. Most everyone had gone by this time, and I just have to guess that Gail was plum out of energy. Mrs. Barstow was actually there waiting for us. We looked and felt like drowned rats.

"What happened?" she asked. We told her we dumped over, sparing her all the embarrassing details. "Are you all OK?" Gosh, I thought no one would ever ask!!!

The season drew quickly to an end, and before we knew it, we were beginning our last race. It would have been Lettie's turn to be skipper, but Gail said we could organize the crew any way we wanted. I suddenly became a monster control freak. This was our last race and I wanted it to be perfect. "Hoist the mainsail up a bit more, it's not tight enough!" I yelled. I put Linda on the jib and then told Lettie where to sit. "I'm taking the tiller and the mainsail!" I announced.

"You can't do both!" Lettie protested.

"Yes, I can and I'm going to!"

I was extremely aggressive on the start, insisting on my right of way, easing out one of the other boats. We crossed the starting line second, which had never happened before. The wind was out of the southeast. Everyone else started on a starboard tack. I took a port tack. "You're going the wrong way!" Linda yelled.

"No, I'm just doing it different." When I came about to a starboard tack, the others were coming about to a port tack. Bobby was ahead, the other two were neck in neck. Just then the wind shifted and suddenly I was pointed straight toward the first buoy. "If we can just hold this tack, we won't have to come about again." And we didn't. I was holding the mainsail tight and we were flying.

"We're going so fast!" screamed Lettie.

"That's the idea!" I yelled back. Because of the shift in wind, we were the first to round the buoy. We rounded it neatly and headed down wind, but it was slow going. We stuck out the mainsail and the jib, but we were moving like molasses. The others weren't moving much either, but they were gaining on us. Then I remembered something I'd read in one of the books called "jibing down wind." We tried it and we picked up speed. We added distance, however, and I sensed the others were going to beat us to the second buoy. Then there was a lull that came over the lake and everyone seemed to stop. "Oh, come on wind!

Don't stop now!" Then there was a funny gust, which caught us beautifully, and we surged forward reaching the second buoy before anyone. The last leg was a beam reach. We were still ahead, but Bobby was closing in on us.

"Pull in on the jib, just a little!" I ordered Linda. "Lettie, sit on the other side!"

"But, . . ."

"Just do it!" It put us at a slightly different angle and we picked up just a bit of speed, just enough to keep our lead. As we neared the finish line, Bobby picked up speed. I saw his grandfather watching with binoculars from the pier with several parents. "Not this time!" I pledged. I pulled the main sail just a tad bit tighter and picked up enough speed to cross the finish line, just about a half a boat length ahead. We couldn't believe it! We'd actually won a race!

When we docked the boat, which we did excellently, several people said, "Good job girls!"

"Fabulous finish!"

"Nice strategy!"

"You used your head!" Yes, they were talking about us, Linda, Lettie and me! The kind lady that had helped Lettie our first day was especially encouraging, and she gave Lettie a big hug when we got off the boat. Bobby's boat had pulled in right beside ours, but his grandfather was gone.

We unrigged the boat quickly and ambled up to the clubhouse to claim our free ice cream cones, which were always awarded to the winning team. We sat on the porch indulging ourselves, rehashing every inch of the race and gloating. Gail came by and told us we did fabulously and that she was proud of us. Really! She really said she was proud of us, and that we'd learned more that summer than anyone else had. Bobby came by and I said, "Hey Champ, great race!" Not the right thing to say, he just glowered at me.

"Yeah, right!" he yelled, with tears in his eyes. Suddenly I felt a tad bit sad for him, but continued to enjoy the victory, the ice cream and my new found friends. Then I heard yelling coming from behind the building. I left the porch, walked through the building and stood at the screen door, eavesdropping. It was Bobby's grandfather.

"What happened to you out there today? What were you thinking about? Not the race, that's for sure! You did so many dumb things! You'll never get to the Olympics like this! You really let us down. How could you let a girl beat you, especially one who doesn't even know how to sail? What's wrong with you? I'm really disappointed in you today, and I know your dad and brother will be just as upset as I am!" And then Cap stormed off toward his car with a crying Bobby trailing behind. I felt just awful for Bobby. Sure, I'd hated him all summer, but I'd had no idea what his grandfather was like! I was almost sorry I'd won.

It was my mom's turn to pick us up. She pulled up, late as always, and asked, "Did you have fun?" At that moment I appreciated her more than I had in a very long time.

"Yeah, Mom, we did! We really did! Thanks for the lessons!"